D1092836

ST HELENS LIBRARIES

3 8055 25002 8551

# Showdown at Squaw Pass

When two drovers are found dead on the Western Trail near the Texas town of Cutter's Crossing, marshals Hank Ross and Abe Naylor aim to find their killers and bring them to justice. But their task is complicated when the local schoolteacher, Alice Carnaby, is kidnapped by the drovers' killer, who heads for Mexico with her. Ross and Naylor join forces with George Bowman, a half-breed Indian tracker, and set out after them.

However, an unscrupulous local rancher has his own reasons for making sure the marshals don't succeed in freeing Alice, and sends four men to kill both her and the marshals. The rancher is determined there will be no witnesses – and therefore no trial. . . .

*By the same author*

Buffalo Falls
Gunfight at Copper Creek

# Showdown at Squaw Pass

Robert B. McNeill

**A Black Horse Western**

ROBERT HALE

© Robert B. McNeill 2017
First published in Great Britain 2017

ISBN 978-0-7198-2495-1

The Crowood Press
The Stable Block
Crowood Lane
Ramsbury
Marlborough
Wiltshire SN8 2HR

www.bhwesterns.com

Robert Hale is an imprint
of The Crowood Press

The right of Robert B. McNeill to be identified as
author of this work has been asserted by him
in accordance with the Copyright, Designs and
Patents Act 1988

All rights reserved. No part of this publication may be
reproduced or transmitted in any form or by any means,
electronic or mechanical, including photocopying, recording,
or any information storage and retrieval system, without
permission in writing from the publishers.

| St Helens Libraries | |
| --- | --- |
| 3 8055 25002 8551 | |
| **Askews & Holts** | 13-Nov-2017 |
| AF | £14.50 |
| | |

# ONE

It was a little after four in the morning when the drive got underway. Two thousand head of cattle trampled the earth and created a massive cloud of dust as they began to move up the trail.

The drover to the rear and left of the milling animals neither saw nor heard his killer approach. Two riders moved out from the cover of a stand of cottonwoods and fell in behind him as he followed the herd across an old watercourse.

The man closest sighted the Sharps .52 and squeezed the trigger. There was a crack as the hammer fell and the cartridge ignited. The bullet smashed into the cowpuncher's back and catapulted him from his saddle into the dried-out stream bed. A drover nearby heard the shot and rode over to investigate, and a second shot rang out and he, too, fell dead.

The shooter dismounted and went to the first man shot, who lay facing the ground. He turned the body over and gave a grunt of satisfaction. 'We got him,' he said to his companion. 'Now let's get the hell out of here.'

Hank Ross reined in his roan gelding and made a cautious descent of the arroyo to where the drovers lay. Two other riders followed, each stepping his horse carefully through the thick mesquite clinging to the banks of the dried-out stream.

The men dismounted and Ross squatted to take a closer look. The dead cowmen were positioned three feet apart, the first lying prone to the creek bottom, the second face up, head and shoulders supported by the rise of the opposite bank.

Ross got to his feet and addressed the fresh-faced youngster, Tom Allinson, who stood beside Abe Naylor. 'Tom, your heard two shots. How long would you say between them?'

The youth looked at the tall deputy and swallowed. In daylight, the spectacle of his dead trail mates and the clear sight of their injuries made him feel queasy. 'Half a minute or so, I guess,' he replied, almost whispering. 'Could've been less.'

'And how long from then until you found the

men lying here?'

'No more than ten minutes.'

At this point the marshal of Cutter's Crossing walked over to the dead cowmen. Abe Naylor was a man in his late forties, heavy set and of medium height. He reached into his waistcoat pockets and brought out a tan leather tobacco pouch and a short-stemmed briar pipe, which he proceeded to fill. He lit the pipe, puffed until he got it going, then said, 'Tom, let me get this straight. You say the two men here are called Pete Bruille and Billy Temple. Three of you were riding drag a little after four this morning when the shooting happened. Now, just to make sure I've got my facts right, take us over everything again from the start, will you?'

'Sure, marshal. Like I said, I'm with the Triple Bar-H ranch. That's near Abilene, Texas. Ed Purvey's the ramrod – the boss of the outfit. He and eleven men, me included, left there three days ago to take 2,500 head of cattle up to Dodge City. Last night we made camp just north of Cutter's Crossing.

'This morning we rose as usual for the 4am chow call, and after breakfast we got underway. Frenchy – that's what we call Bruille – Billy Temple and me were riding drag; you know, in back of the steers? One of us rides at either side of the herd and one in the middle.

'Apart from Purvey, the cook and the remuda man – the hand who looks after the spare horses – there's six other men, three on each flank. Two of 'em, point riders, ride up front, and they're followed by two swing riders between the point riders and the halfway mark. The next two – flank men – ride halfway between the swing and drag positions.

'As I told you, I was riding right drag, with Billy in the centre and Bruille on the left. When I heard the first shot there would have been about a quarter of a mile between me and Frenchy.

'When I heard the shot we were crossing the creek. It was still full dark and I thought he was having trouble with the steers. You know, tangled up in mesquite brush or something?'

'Yes, go on,' Naylor said.

'We usually only shoot to attract attention if we get in a fix. Trail boss doesn't like it otherwise. It can spook the herd and cause a stampede. Anyway, Billy calls over, says he's going to take a look. Then a short while later I heard another shot.'

Ross said, 'That one also coming from here?'

'Yeah, so I rode up to my flank man – Jim Grierson – and told him to cover my position while I took a look.'

'And that's when you found them,' said Naylor.

8

Allinson glanced hesitantly in the direction of his dead companions. The sick feeling had eased a little while he'd been talking, but now it returned. 'Yes,' he replied.

'I know this can't be easy for you, Tom,' said Ross. 'Just another couple of minutes and we'll let you catch up with the drive. Did you see anyone either prior to the shots or afterward?'

'No,' Allinson replied. 'When the shots were fired the entire herd was rolling. It's pretty noisy. Likely that would mask the sound of anyone riding away.'

Naylor raised his right boot and tapped the pipe against the heel, dislodging ash. 'Anyone else hear or see anything?'

'No,' Allinson replied. 'After I found the men I went straight to Ed Purvey. He asked everyone, but though most heard shots, nobody saw anything. He told me then to ride back to Cutter's Crossing and tell what happened.'

Ross stroked his chin. 'Did any of you visit town last night?'

'Yeah,' Allinson said. 'I think Ed Purvey let some of the men go for a few beers.'

'Any trouble while they were there that you know of?'

'I did hear of some argument at the saloon. One

of the card tables, I think.'

'Involving Bruille and Temple?' asked Ross.

'I'm not sure,' Allinson said. 'I didn't go to town myself.'

'OK, Tom,' Naylor said. 'You can get on and catch up with your outfit. Oh, and ask Ed Purvey to call at my office on his way back from Dodge in case there's anything else I need to ask. By the way – these men's horses still here?'

'Yes,' Allinson replied. 'They're in a pasture over the next rise. Both hobbled.'

'Fine,' Naylor said. 'Before you go, fetch one back and we'll take these men to town for burying. Purvey can collect it on his return.'

As the young drover rode off, Naylor turned to Ross. 'What do you think, Hank,' he asked. 'Rustlers caught in the act?'

'Possible, I guess. Robbery could be a motive, too, even though only one thing appears to be missing – and that from the first man shot.'

'Oh,' Naylor said, 'What's that?'

'Bruille's pistol – it's not in his holster.'

# TWO

Cutter's Crossing was similar to dozens of towns that sprang up on the Texas prairies in the years following the Civil War. Like others that boomed on the beef trade, it was pretty basic in the beginning: a collection of tents and shacks set up to see to the needs of men on the Western Trail. By 1874, however, the cattle trade had grown apace, and the town had grown with it. The bustling main street was now over a half mile in length, and the diverse range of businesses occupying its frontage included an eighty-room hotel, a dry goods emporium, and a ladies' milliner offering the latest in Eastern fashions.

Back at the marshal's office, Naylor and Ross discussed the drovers' killings and considered possible motives. The marshal stuck to his theory that the shootings had been carried out by would-be cattle thieves. He was convinced Bruille had been shot confronting a gang of rustlers. Naylor said it was likely the cowhand had come upon them trying to separate steers from the herd and, when challenged, had been shot at point-black range. Temple had heard the shot, and when he went to investigate, had been killed in turn.

'Still don't explain why they took the man's gun,' Ross said.

'It's possible he lost it.'

'True, but it's rare for a cowhand to get parted from his six-gun.' Ross was thinking of an ordinance prohibiting the carrying of guns within town limits. On arrival, all weapons were meant to be left with either himself or Naylor and collected on departure. A town statute allowed a fine of anything up to fifty dollars for such offences. Few trail men took any notice, however. Ross recalled several occasions when he'd confronted drunken drovers – some just boisterous but others who'd become threatening – to enforce the order.

'Well, you could be right, Hank,' said Naylor. 'Don't rightly know why anyone would shoot a man for a pistol, though – and that's the only thing that looks to be missing. Seems the only lead we've got is that there was an argument at the saloon. Go over and check with Nate Peacock. See what you come up with.'

Ross pushed the batwing doors and entered Peacock's Saloon. He stood for a moment to let his eyes adjust to the light from the oil lamps. Although there was bright sunshine outside, the few windows in the bar admitted little natural light.

Nate Peacock stood behind the counter drying a tumbler with a cloth so grimy that Ross thought the glass was likely to be dirtier now than when it left the water. 'Howdy, Hank,' he said. 'What can I get you?'

Ross acknowledged the saloon keeper with a nod, then looked around. His eyes were accustomed to the darkness now and he noticed there were only two customers, both seated at one of the saloon's plain wooden tables. 'Nothing, Nate. Seems you could use more custom, though.'

'Oh, it's just a lull. Time for a breather. Two outfits were in last night – packed the place to the rafters. Another big herd due through tomorrow.' Peacock put the glass down bottom side up, then spread his hands on the counter. 'Some kinda problem, Hank?'

Ross was aware news travelled fast in Cutter's Crossing. Most citizens would have now heard

13

about the men brought back for burial earlier that day. 'It's about the two cattlemen shot dead on the trail five miles north of town. Young drover who found them says there was a disturbance here last night. Some argument over cards.'

'Two cowhands killed on the trail?' Peacock said. 'Hadn't heard that. Yeah, there was an incident at one of the tables. Got knocked over in the middle of a faro game. Some 'poke got all liquored up and swayed into it. Everything spilled to the floor. My barman Murphy gave the bum a taste of night air.'

'That all there was to it?'

'Yeah, the guy had had a snootful. I'm sure he was one of Tom Morgan's hands – headed south only this morning if you want to talk to him.'

Ross tapped a forefinger to the brim of his hat and turned to leave. 'Thanks.'

'What were the dead men's names, Hank?' asked Peacock.

'Bruille and Temple. Know them?'

'Temple, no. Bruille – good looking, tall?'

'Yes, that would fit the description.'

'I think he was better known by his nickname – Frenchy, on account of his accent? Saw him in here last night, too. Playin' faro, I think. Helluva pleasant guy, always said "please" and "thank you" when I served him. I hear tell he was a bit of a ladies' man.'

Ross stood on the boardwalk outside the saloon wondering why the two Triple Bar-H men had met their deaths. He was positive the motive wasn't rustling. For one thing the shooting had taken place *after* breakfast. Ross thought it more likely for cattle thieves to have struck earlier, when the drovers were asleep. Although many outfits kept a few men on picket duty at night, he doubted that this was true in the Triple Bar-H's case. Their crew numbered only twelve men, a figure that included the cook and trail boss. To function on a drive, every man needed his rest. He didn't think an outfit with twelve men could afford to post much of a watch.

Moreover, the outfit had camped at night near Cutter's Crossing. A professional rustling outfit would have chosen to raid further along the trail – someplace where there was less likelihood of local lawmen being alerted and a posse put together.

Then there was the way the men had been killed: one shot in the back and one in the chest. Ross believed that Bruille, the first man shot, had been deliberately targeted. Temple had arrived at the scene almost immediately. He'd seen the shooter, and had been shot dead as a result.

The killer or killers thwarted any prospect of being tracked, too. He or they simply rode in the hoofprints made by two thousand longhorn steers. But Ross recognized that this fact also presented the strongest clue to the killer's whereabouts, as the tracks went only two ways. With the sun rising soon, he could have gone either north, and taken the risk of being seen by the Triple Bar-H hands, or in one other direction. And that seemed the more likely: south to Cutter's Crossing.

Ross stepped down from the boardwalk and began to cross the street. He had almost gained the halfway mark when he heard a pistol being cocked behind him.

'Hold it right there, deputy,' a voice said. 'Keep your hands high and stay facing forward. Move a muscle and I'll shoot.'

Ross stopped dead in his tracks but kept his arms still. He was sure he knew the voice, and swung his head until he could see an outline of the man in his peripheral vision. 'OK Stu, that's enough,' he said, turning to face the gunman. 'Holster the pistol.'

'Had you for a minute though, didn't I, Hank?' The man began to laugh. 'Thought you were going to wet your boots. Just as well it was me – an outlaw would have plugged you, for sure.' The speaker was Stu Naylor, son of the town marshal. He was nineteen, stockily built like his father, with flaxen hair that ended well below his collar.

Ross felt a flash of anger and almost lashed out at the young man. He kept his temper in check only out of respect to the memory of Abe Naylor's late wife, Marion, who'd been taken with consumption seven years before.

It seemed to Ross that any shred of decency the boy possessed had been buried with his mother, as Stu's malevolent streak had manifested itself the week after Marion was laid to rest.

The twelve-year-old had taken his father's Henry rifle, climbed a mesa overlooking the trail a mile south of town, and awaited the arrival of the Boone & Bannerman stage. The Concord was rounding a bend pulled by a team of six when the youngster ruthlessly dropped the two lead horses in their traces, causing the big coach to overturn. Luckily no one was killed, though one man broke his arm and another was laid up for three weeks with a torn ligament.

Marion's recent death and the fact that Stu was a minor influenced the Citizen's Committee towards clemency. Abe Naylor also promised to discipline his son, and gave an assurance that the boy would be strictly supervised from that day forth.

Despite this, it wasn't long before Stu was again

in trouble. Ross recalled that in a fight with another boy at the schoolhouse – an attack the teacher swore was unprovoked – Stu had taken a pocket knife and removed a piece of his adversary's ear. In the years since then Stu Naylor's maverick nature had caused him to be involved in any number of fist fights. Fortunately, except for the stage incident, no event since had involved a gun. In the light of what was happening now, however, Ross thought it could only be a matter of time.

Ross walked two paces to where Stu Naylor stood. He put out his hand and gestured for the pistol. 'You know the town ordinance regarding guns,' he said. 'Give it to me.'

Stu had complied with Ross's instruction and re-holstered the gun. But now he hooked his thumbs inside his gunbelt and stuck out his chin in a gesture of defiance. 'Hell, Hank, you know I was only funnin'. I ain't gonna give up my gun to you or anybody.'

'The fact you're the marshal's son don't put you above the law, Stewart. Town statutes apply to you same as anyone else. Now, you gonna give me the gun, or do I have to take it?'

Stu withdrew his right hand from his gun belt and positioned it over the holster. 'Think you're quicker on the draw, Hank?'

Ross didn't reply. Instead, in one swift and fluid movement, he moved a fraction to the left and hooked his right heel behind the young man's right ankle. He then swung right and thrust his shoulder into his opponent, causing him to pitch backwards. Stu gasped, and as he fell, Ross reached out and snatched his pistol from its holster.

Ross stood over Stu, who now sat on his backside regarding the deputy with stunned surprise. 'OK, Stu. You've a choice: sass me some more and pay a visit to the hoosegow, or go home peaceably without another word. Make up your mind.'

Stu got to his feet, his face scarlet with anger. He gave Ross a cold, hard stare, then opened his mouth as if to speak.

Ross stopped him short. 'Just one word, Stu – your choice.'

Stu picked up his hat, turned on his heel, and walked to the rail where his bay was tethered. He untied the reins, stuck his hat back on his head, mounted and made ready to leave.

'I'll check in this pistol at the jailhouse, Stu,' said Ross, 'where it should have been to begin with. Oh, and by the way – it's confiscated for seven days. You can pick it up any time after then. On your way out of town, of course.'

Stu spurred the bay, who whinnied and moved

off at a gallop. The marshal's son waited until he was just out of earshot, then muttered under his breath, 'Your time's coming, Ross. Soon ... very damned soon.'

Guenther Hartmann was approaching Cutter's Crossing on his grey with his pack pony in tow when the marshal's son passed him at full gallop. Hartmann tipped a forefinger to his hat, but the young man rode on without acknowledgement. Stewart Naylor was a strange boy, Hartmann thought, so very unlike his father. But then, there was much that was strange here in the New World.

For all that, Hartmann mused, it was amazing how quickly he'd gotten used to the country. Looking back now he found it hard to believe it had only been six years since he'd sailed from Bremen to Maryland.

Hartmann started by taking advantage of the demand for photographs on the weekly cattle drives. Drovers were constantly changing on the trail, and there were always new cowmen keen to have a likeness made to give to sweethearts and families.

Three days every week for four years, Hartmann had loaded his heavy wooden camera and equipment on his pony to take pictures of trail hands who, when paid in Dodge City at the end of the drive, would set aside a few dollars and collect the photographs on their way south. Hartmann's business had proved so profitable that by 1872 – only two years after setting up – he'd been able to buy the property in Cutter's Crossing that housed his studio. Since then the people of the town and surrounding community had also embraced the medium that enabled them to have a permanent record of christenings, engagements, weddings, anniversaries and the like.

Indeed, in the last six months Hartmann had prospered to the point where he had been able to pay the passage for his sister's son, Erich, who journeyed from his native Heidelberg to become his assistant. It was a wise move, as Erich proved himself to be an exceptionally capable young man, so much so that Hartmann was able to leave the day-to-day running of the studio to his nephew when he himself travelled the Western Trail.

Hartmann was still in the middle of his reverie and unpacking his pony when he was startled by a voice from behind.

'Mornin' Guenther. Busy trip?'

Hartmann looked round in and saw the deputy marshal leaning on a post at the boardwalk. The photographer smiled. Hank Ross had been one of the first to extend a welcoming hand when he arrived at Cutter's Crossing, and Hartmann considered him a friend. 'Yes, Hank, thank you. This time I journeyed as far south as Sutter's Falls and photographed cowmen from three big outfits. And now I have my nephew Erich develop the negatives to make pictures for the men to collect on their return.'

'Those outfits you took pictures of, Guenther. They include Triple Bar-H men?'

'Triple Bar-H, Hank? I'm not sure ...'

'Ed Purvey's outfit?'

Hartmann kneaded his forehead in concentration. 'Ed Purvey ... Edward Purvey, yes! I met him and his drovers a few miles north of Sutter's Falls.'

Ross stepped down from the boardwalk. 'Did all Purvey's men have their picture taken?'

Hartmann unstrapped a heavy wooden tripod and lifted it clear of the pony. 'I think so, Hank,' he said, slightly winded by the effort. 'The names of all who have been photographed are in my notebook. Why do you ask?'

'Just a hunch, Guenther. Here, let me take that for you.'

A few minutes later Hartmann and Ross stood at either side of a large oak desk in the studio's reception area. Hartmann leafed through a thick lined notebook and pointed to a page. 'This is my record book, Hank; Herr Purvey's men's names are on this page.'

'Will you see if you've taken a picture of a man by the name of Bruille. B-R-U-I-L-L-E, I think it's spelt.'

Hartmann took a pair of wire-framed glasses from his waistcoat, put them on, and ran a forefinger down the page. 'Let me see: Danvers; Taylor; Hodgkiss – ah, here we are – Brool. Sorry, Hank, my English is not good. I think I've spelt it wrong.'

'Don't matter,' Ross said. 'It must be the same guy. Can you show me his picture?'

'But of course, Hank. I'll have my nephew process the negatives straightaway.'

'How long will it take?'

'Oh, less than an hour, I think.'

'Good. Let me give you a hand to bring in the rest of your gear, and I'll explain why I need your help.'

An hour later a fair-haired young man entered the reception room carrying a tray of prints. Hartmann, who was seated with Ross, rose to introduce his nephew. 'Ach, so. Hank, this is my sister's boy, Erich. He has been with me four months now.'

The young man put the tray on the desk, then shook Ross's hand. 'Very pleased to meet you, sir.'

'Likewise, Erich,' Ross said, then pointed to the

prints. 'These turn out OK?'

'Oh yes, sir,' Erich replied. 'Every one a perfect exposure.'

Hartmann indicated the prints. 'Please, Hank, examine them and see if you can find what you're looking for.'

Ross rose and leafed through the pile of sepia-toned photographs. The images were similar: young men, mostly in their late teens and early twenties, pictured with the open range in the background. In some of the photographs, however, Ross noted a chuck wagon had been used as a backdrop. Most of the men stood, though some crouched or sat cross-legged. All were dressed pretty much the same: knee-length boots with raised heels; outer-wear that included leather chaps and waistcoat; a heavy cotton shirt, usually checked; a bandanna knotted below the neck; and, in almost every picture, a wide-brimmed hat.

Ross saw, too, that each man proudly posed with his sidearm on show. In most pictures this was a Colt single-action army .45, known as the Peacemaker. But there were other makes also, such as Smith & Wesson and Remington.

After studying a dozen or so prints, Ross came to the one he was looking for. He almost failed to rec-ognize Bruille: in life the man did indeed stand out from the other drovers, with a dark, Latin complexion that complemented a wide, handsome face.

Ross studied the print for a moment, tapped it with his finger, then said, 'This is definitely the man, Guenther. But I'd particularly like a closer view of one area of the picture. You got a magnifying glass?'

Hartmann opened the top drawer of his desk. 'Sure, Hank, sure. Here, try this.'

Ross took the glass and placed it over the area he wanted to examine, then pulled it back until he found focus. In the picture, Bruille's gun was clearly defined in its holster. It was a pistol Ross had not often come across: a Deane-Adams five-cylinder model with a pearl handle. And this was the second time today he'd seen the weapon.

The first had been two hours earlier when he'd taken it from Stu Naylor.

# THREE

Ross strode along the boardwalk on Main Street and came to a door over which was a sign bearing the legend TOWN MARSHAL. He entered the office and saw an attractive young woman seated at Abe Naylor's desk. She was in her early twenties, of slight build, and wore her dark hair up and pinned beneath a lace-fringed hat. Ross noted she'd been crying.

Abe Naylor rose from behind the desk. 'Hank, I like to introduce Miss Alice ...' He frowned in an effort to recall the woman's surname.

'Carnaby,' the woman said, offering her hand.

Ross took it and raised his hat in greeting. 'Hank Ross. Pleased to meet you, ma'am.'

'Miss Carnaby came to see us in connection with

the death of Pete Bruille,' Naylor said. 'She says she knows who the killer is.'

Alice Carnaby dabbed the corner of a handkerchief to her eye. 'As I was explaining to the marshal, it all began six weeks ago when I met Jed Transome at the cattleman's dance.'

Jed Transome, Ross recalled, was the son of Elias Transome, one of the community's richest and most influential citizens, who owned a large spread ten miles west of town. Transome had several business interests in Cutter's Crossing, which included the Cattleman's Bank and the Imperial Hotel. It was also rumoured he'd recently bought shares in a railroad company that planned to run a spur to the town.

'Jed asked to see me the following week and I agreed,' Alice continued. 'He picked me up in his buckboard and we went for a drive in the country. We stopped for a picnic at Indian Rock, you know, where the river forks? Anyway, he was agreeable company and we had a pleasant outing. He behaved like a gentleman throughout – at no time did he press his attentions or anything like that.

'He took me home afterward and I thanked him. I thought him a likeable young man, but I must emphasize I had no romantic attraction to him whatsoever. The meeting had been pleasant but strictly platonic for me, and I assumed Jed felt the same way.

'I thought no more about it until a week later when a package was delivered to my home. I opened it to reveal an emerald ring that was accompanied by a note, which said: "To my Darling Alice, to seal our Engagement. My undying Love and Devotion, Jedidiah Transome."

'I sent the ring back immediately, of course, and included a letter that explained in no uncertain terms that his sentiments were absolutely unrequited. I heard no more from him and I thought that was the end of it.

'Then the day before yesterday I was riding Jack, my Appaloosa, back from town when a storm came up. Jack was frightened by a sudden thunderclap – he threw me and bolted. I had sprained my ankle quite badly and I couldn't move for a while. Luckily, I was rescued by Mr Bruille and another drover who were riding south from town with supplies for their outfit. The other drover went after Jack, and Mr Bruille was helping me on his horse when Jed happened by.

'He asked what was going on and Mr Bruille said to him, "This lady has been thrown from her horse, *Monsieur*, who was panicked in the storm. She has been hurt and I am taking her home."

'It was then that Jed became enraged and seemed to lose all reason. He swore at Mr Bruille and shouted, "You're goin' nowhere, Frog swine – don't you know that's my fiancée you're manhandling! Put her down, pronto. If anyone takes her home, it'll be me."

'At this point I became angry myself. I told Jed he was a misguided fool and that he and I were not engaged, nor would ever be. Mr Bruille said, "You heard the lady, *Monsieur*. Now I ask you – please – step aside, I intend taking her home."

'Jed went for his pistol, but the second he did so a gun was already in the Frenchman's hand. He said to Jed, "I don't want to shoot you, *Monsieur*. But if you force me I will. Now please, rein your horse to one side and let us proceed".

'Jed seemed surprised, humiliated and angry all at the same time. He said to Mr Bruille, "I won't forget this, mister. Next time we meet you better pray you see me coming. 'Cause if you don't, I'm gonna make sure it's the day you draw your last breath".'

'I take it Jed allowed you and Bruille to carry on at that point,' Ross said.

Alice put the handkerchief back in her purse. 'Oh yes. He was still angry, of course. Very angry. But he just turned his horse and rode away.'

29

'And Pete Bruille got you home safely without further trouble?' Ross said.

'Yes.'

Naylor rubbed his chin. 'Pardon me for askin' ma'am, but had you met Bruille before that day – and did you see him again after?'

'No, I hadn't – and I didn't. I was someone in trouble, Marshal, and Mr Bruille showed me an act of kindness. When we arrived at my place, naturally I thanked him, and, since it was still raining hard, I offered him coffee. He declined, though, saying he had to join up with his outfit. His friend arrived at that moment and returned Jack to me, then both men left.'

'Well, I reckon that's all we need for the moment, Miss Carnaby,' said Naylor. 'You've been very helpful. If we need to ask anything else, where can we find you?'

'My cabin is over on Pine Road, behind the schoolhouse. I'm the teacher there.'

'You're the lady from Baltimore who replaced Miss Tate, who retired in April?' Ross asked.

Alice smiled at Ross. 'Yes,' she replied.

Ross looked slightly abashed. 'Ah . . . well, like I mentioned earlier, ma'am, it's a pleasure to make your acquaintance.'

Alice Carnaby left the office and Naylor went

over to the middle of the room and opened the door of a wood-burning stove. He took a spill from a tin box, lit it, and began puffing his pipe. He looked at Ross. It was evident his deputy was still thinking about the young woman. Naylor paused and said, 'She's a pretty one, ain't she?'

'Huh? Oh, yes. Yes, she certainly is.'

Ross remembered the photograph then, and the bad news he had for his boss. 'Miss Carnaby's information certainly seems to point to the killer. There's something else, though. I hate to have to say it, Abe, but it's something that affects you personally.'

'You're sure about this?' said Naylor. He and Ross were standing at the marshal's desk, on which was a copy of Bruille's photograph, together with the Deane-Adams revolver.

'The evidence speaks for itself, Abe. Sorry.'

Naylor sighed. 'It's the pistol in the photograph, sure enough – you don't often see that model. And you took it off Stu this morning?'

'Just like I told you, Abe.'

'Then how the hell does that square with what that schoolmarm told us? C'mon, you and I are gonna ride out to my place and have a word with that boy.'

'We was havin' a shootin' contest,' said Stu Naylor, who stood at one end of a large stone fireplace with his father standing opposite. 'Early this mornin', 'fore I had my run in with Ross. Jed Transome bet me the Deane-Adams he could shoot the most corks off a row of bottles. Best of six shots. I got four, him two. I won the gun fair and square.'

Abe Naylor turned the Deane-Adams in his hand, and gestured towards his son with the butt end. 'And where did *he* get it?'

'Told me he'd won it in a hand of poker last night. Peacock's saloon.'

'Did he say who he won it from?' Ross said.

Stu Naylor gave Ross a look of contempt. 'Frenchy. Don't know his last name. One of Purvey's men.'

Abe Naylor gave his son a cold, hard look. 'You sassed my deputy this mornin', Stu. Now you're doin' it again. Hank and I are goin' to Transome's place now and see if what you and he says tallies. If it don't, and I find you're lyin', I swear I'll take a switch to your rump, big as you are. Don't you make a move till we get back, you hear?'

'Yes . . .' Stu looked toward the hearth then raised his head, caught the determined glint in his father's eye, and added, '. . . sir.'

Elias Transome's place was a substantial two-storey ranch house made of weathered limestone. The property was situated on a slight rise, in front of which was a corral where five men were gathered. Four of the men stood on the outside of the fence watching a fifth, who was inside attempting to rope an unbroken stallion. As the marshal and his deputy rode through the gate, one of the watchers, a large man with a beard, detached himself from the others and waved a hand, signalling Ross and Naylor to stop.

As the lawmen reined their mounts, the man strode over and grabbed the halter of Naylor's grey. He then looked at the marshal and said, 'What do you want?'

Naylor pulled back his waistcoat to reveal his star. 'Abe Naylor, marshal of Cutter's Crossing. This here's my deputy, Hank Ross. We've come to see Jed Transome.'

The man was in his late thirties and had a scar that traversed his face from the corner of his right eye to his upper lip. He tightened his grip on the horse's headstall. 'What do you want to see him about?'

'I don't know who you are,' Naylor replied. 'My

business is with Jed Transome. Now why don't you tell me where he's at?'

'I'm the foreman in charge here, and I decide who gets to see Mr Transome – and his boy. Marshal or not, you're on private land. You gonna say why you want to see my boss's son, or do I have you run off the property?'

Ross said, 'We're pursuing county business, mister. I'd advise your co-operation, else risk a charge of obstruction.'

The foreman swung toward Ross and moved his hand toward his holster. 'Obstruction? You threatenin' me, deputy?'

'Take your hand away from that gunbelt, mister, or I'll be mighty tempted to shoot you. That ain't no threat.' The foreman had only taken his eyes from Naylor for a moment, but it had been enough time for the marshal to draw his rifle and place the muzzle of its barrel next to the big man's ear.

'What's going on here, Everett?' The speaker stood just a few feet away. He was a man in his mid-fifties, greying at the temples, and his stentorian tone of voice gave the impression of authority.

'Man here's marshal of Cutter's Crossing and this is his deputy, Mr Transome. Said they wanted a word. I was just tryin' to find out why. Didn't want to bother you with anythin' trivial.'

'Ah, well. Sorry, marshal. Deputy. Hobbs here is charged with looking after my privacy. I'm afraid he can sometimes be a little over-protective. Why do you want to see me?'

Abe Naylor replaced the Winchester in its scabbard. 'It's not you we want to speak to, Mr Transome, it's your son.'

'Why . . . why do you want to speak to Jed?'

'It's not maybe something we should discuss out here.'

'Oh, I see.' Transome turned to Hobbs, 'Where's Jed?'

'Over at the stable, Mr Transome. I think he's groomin' his paint.'

Transome nodded and motioned in the stable's direction. 'Go and fetch him.' Then, turning to Ross and Naylor, he said, 'Perhaps you gentlemen would care to come inside?'

'Why, the whole thing's outrageous,' Transome said. He was standing beside a large oak table in the middle of his study, a room crammed with fancy furniture and fittings. Ross guessed the carpet was Persian, and the huge bookcase looked to be made out of something solid like cherry or rosewood. The plush chairs around the table were probably French, as was the sofa with arms that angled outward at either end. Paintings and carved-frame mirrors covered the walls, and other items included a writing desk, a long-case clock, and a glass-fronted drinks cabinet complete with crystal decanters.

'Sorry, Mr Transome,' Naylor said, 'the school-teacher said your boy threatened to shoot Bruille. I don't think the lady's gonna lie about a thing like that.'

'Well,' Transome replied, 'that's something that would have to be decided in a court of law. After all, it's only her word against Jed's. And with regard to the Deane-Adams, you mentioned your boy said Jed came by the gun in a poker game.'

Ross cleared his throat. 'Ah well, we were comin' to that . . '

Naylor interrupted. 'Seems my son's been lyin', Mr Transome. We checked again with Nate Peacock before we came out here. He saw Bruille playing faro with some others last night, but swears your son never came near the place.'

'He might have won it off the man at a game somewhere else,' said Transome.

Ross said, 'No sir, he couldn't have. Peacock remembers Bruille being at the table all evenin'. Besides, why would he and Jed want to sit down together after the argument over Miss Carnaby?'

At that moment there was a knock on the door,

and Everett Hobbs entered. 'It's about Jed, Mr Transome,' he said.

'Yes?'

'He's not in the stable, sir. Neither's the paint. The horse's been saddled . . . Jed's gone.'

# FOUR

Stu Naylor became increasingly restless waiting in the house. Less than an hour after his father and Ross rode off, he walked to the stable, saddled his bay, and cantered over to a meadow a mile from the house. A family of prairie dogs had excavated a series of tunnels in a rise at the far end, and Stu often went there to stalk the animals and kill them.

He dismounted, crouched low behind a rock, and awaited his prey. His eye was sighted along the barrel of his father's old .44 Henry carbine when he saw two small furry bodies leave their burrow and scamper the short distance between two earthen mounds.

He drew a bead on the animal behind, and was increasing pressure on the Henry's trigger when he heard the hammer of a pistol being cocked at his back. A voice said, 'Looks like they're not the only rodents round here.'

Stu jumped and took a sharp breath. The Henry bucked in his hands. The bullet hit a cottonwood tree on the other side of the prairie dogs, splintering the bark and making them dart for the nearest hole. Stu glanced behind him. 'Jed! You shouldn't sneak up on a fella like that. I near jumped out my skin.'

Jed Transome was a full six years older than Naylor, a tall, thin young man whose blue-grey eyes betrayed no hint of emotion. 'You've picked the very word I was thinkin' of, Stu. Though I think "sneak" applies to you a bit more'n me, don't you think?'

Stu gulped. Jed now had the revolver pointed at his forehead. 'I – I don't know what you mean, Jed.'

'Don't ya, pard? OK, let me see if I can't wise you up a little. See, there's me at home in the stable combin' Napoleon's mane – you know my paint's called Napoleon, don't you, Stu?'

The younger man nodded.

'Yeah, well, I sees your daddy over at the corral, and he's got that long drink o' water deputy with him, called Ross? Yeah, well they go into the house then, and I eavesdrops. And it seems both of them are there to see me about the death of that Frog.

39

'Yeah well, OK, I know I said in front of Alice I was gonna kill him. But my fiancée don't matter 'cause there was no witnesses there at the time.

'No, it all comes down to the Deane-Adams I let a certain person win for helpin' rid me of that no-good cowpuncher. And howdya think they got to suspectin' me? Well, it seems the same fool let himself get tangled with the law and got the piece taken off him. Now, ain't that a dumb thing?

'So, when he's asked where he got it, what do you think he said? Why, I won it in a contest with Jed . . . shootin' corks offa bottles. Well, I ask you Stu, you had a friend done a dirty trick such as that, what d'you think you would do with him?'

Stu said, 'That's not the way it was, Jed, honest it wasn't. I told 'em you won the pistol off the guy in a poker game.'

Jed snorted derisively. 'Yeah, and I'm likely to get in a game with the Frog after our set-to over Alice. No, it sounds kinda weak to me. 'Sides, there's this guy takin' pictures of them drovers on the trail. Hell if he don't take one of the Frog showin' his holstered Deane-Adams. They know the gun's his, Stu, no doubt about it. Seems they've a pile of evidence that's gettin' bigger by the minute.

'Then there's you, pard. Well, you were there when I shot the guy, weren't you? Why, you're the best witness they could have. I can hear you now: "Jed and me rode after Ed Purvey's drive and waited till the drovers rose just a little before sun up. When they set to movin', Jed shot the man in the back. Then, a little later, when his sidekick came to see what the shootin' was about, Jed shot him too".'

Stu was now almost in tears. 'But don't you see, Jed, I went along 'cause I wanted to. After you told me that Frenchman was tryin' to steal your fiancée, set her against you, I was as angry as you were. You're my pard, Jed, always was. A slight agin' you is a slight agin' me. When Pa and Ross find out I was there with you of my own free will, they'll come after me, too. If you're a wanted man, so am I. It's something they call 'cessory after the fact. I'm as guilty as you are, Jed.'

Jed smiled thinly, then scratched his ear with the muzzle of the .45. 'Ever been to Mexico, Stu?'

'No, Jed. Why?'

Jed reached into his jacket and took out a bulging drawstring pouch. He threw it to Stu, who heard the distinct jingle of coins as he caught it.

'What's in the bag, Jed?'

'Open it and find out.'

Stu opened the pouch and beheld an unmistakable yellow gleam. 'Aren't them gold coins? There looks to be a fortune in here.'

41

'Yeah, them's double eagles. Each worth twenty bucks. There's a hundred of them, my friend, two thousand dollars' worth.'

'Where'd you get 'em, Jed?'

'My pa's safe. Took them early this mornin'. Oh, he won't mind, it's a drop in the ocean to him. I'm headin' for Mexico – makin' a new start. I intend bein' a ranchero down there. That's Mex for ranch owner, Stu. There's a whole heap o' money to be made.

'I'm takin' my fiancée with me, too.' He laughed. 'Of course, she don't know it yet ... and might need a little persuadin'. But I'm sure she'll come round to my way of thinkin'. Thing is, Stu, I'm gonna need a pard to help me get started. You willin'?'

Stu beamed with excitement. 'You bet, Jed. You bet.'

Abe Naylor came out of the house as Ross was checking his roan's cinch. The marshal appeared perplexed, and raised his hands in a show of exasperation. 'No, he ain't in back, either, Hank.'

'What about the meadow you told me he uses for target practice?'

'That's the one we passed on the way in,' Naylor replied, 'where the cottonwoods line the stream.'

'You're sure he hasn't taken anything – apart from his bay?'

'Yeah, he just seems to have saddled his horse. As far as I can tell his clothes' chest and wardrobe ain't been touched.'

'That meadow where he goes to practise his shooting, Abe. I think it might be worth taking a closer look.'

A few minutes later Ross and Naylor stood at the rock Stu had used when stalking the prairie dogs. Ross saw a glint of metal, stooped, and picked up a spent cartridge. He raised it to his nose and sniffed. 'He's been here all right, it's a shell from a .44. Fired recently, I'd say.' Ross studied the ground more carefully. 'Look here, Abe, hoofprints – there's two sets.'

Naylor said, 'You thinkin' what I'm thinkin'?'

'Stu and Jed Transome? Yeah, maybe. It seems too much of a coincidence for them both to go missin' at the same time.'

'You think my boy's mixed up in Bruille's killing?'

'Goin' by what we know, Abe, I'd say without doubt Transome's the killer. It's possible Stu knows something about it, though. Maybe Jed persuaded him it was serious and that's what made him run. You know if he and Transome were friends?'

43

'No, I don't, Hank. Hell, you know in this job I'm in town most days, don't get to spend as much time with him as I should. I ain't deludin' myself, though – I'm sure he gets to mixin' with dubious company in Peacock's and other places. Truth is, I thought I'd been successful at keepin' a lid on his errant ways, but I knows in my heart that ain't true.' Naylor swallowed and his eyes moistened. 'I reckon a boy needs a mother's influence as much as a father's. And of course since Marion died that's somethin' that's been missin' in his life.'

Ross said, 'You've nothin' to reproach yourself for, Abe. You done all anyone could expect.'

Naylor shrugged. 'Well, it seems it ain't been enough. C'mon, Hank, it's time we got to trackin' that pair.'

Elias Transome took a cigar from the humidor on his desk and struck a match. Everett Hobbs stood a respectful distance from his employer, held his hat at his waist, and drummed his fingers nervously on the brim. Transome drew on the cigar, savoured the rich Cuban tobacco on his palate, then blew out the smoke and motioned in the foreman's direction. 'Hobbs, that marshal and his deputy have evidence that links Jed to the death of a drover named Bruille. It appears my son lost his head over some schoolmarm he's been mooning about this past month or so – you know who she is?'

'Yes, Mr Transome. I think the woman's called Carnaby, she's the one that took over from old Miss Tate.'

'Hmm, well anyway, Jed and Bruille had some spat over her, she rejected him, and Jed seems to have lost it – he's quick to anger, got the Irish blood in him from his late mother, Megan.

'It appears Jed followed the man's outfit and shot the fellow as the drive got underway this morning. I don't doubt for a minute the cowpuncher had it coming to him, however. Even though the marshal and his deputy claim the man was shot in the back, and another drover who came to back him up was shot, too.

'Now, in spite of seemingly damning evidence, I dare say I'd have been able to get my lawyer to figure some loophole and get my boy off the hook. But, as you know, the young fool's gone on the run – something any court's going to treat as an admission of guilt. I've also discovered he's taken two thousand dollars in gold coin from my safe. But the money's not what I'm worried about.'

Transome paused and tapped ash into a large marble ashtray. 'Hobbs, you remember that meeting in Dodge you accompanied me to last month?

45

Hobbs shifted his weight to the opposite foot. 'Yes, Mr Transome. When you went to meet the rail-road people?'

'That's it. I secured a twenty per cent stake in a spur that will make Cutter's Crossing the new Dodge City within a few years of completion.

'But the men I met there are not only railroad investors. No, indeed. Each and every one of them has the power to influence things at the very highest level. At the risk of blowing my horn, the kudos I've won with these men is a lot more impor-tant to me than mere railroad investment. What I'm going to tell you now must be treated in the strictest confidence, you understand?'

'Sure thing, Mr Transome.'

'Good. I know I can trust you, Hobbs, but I had to have your word on it. You've been with me a long time and have helped smooth over a few rough patches. We both understand that out here not all things are easy; on the frontier sometimes the only way to get what you want is at the point of a gun.

'What I want to tell you is this: these men I spoke to have put my name forward for the Texas state elections in 1876. I'm running for governor, Hobbs – and they expect me to win. But that's just the beginning. In a few years I intend taking a crack at the White House itself.

'But here's my problem: if Jed's put on trial and found guilty, and word gets to my backers, they're going to act as if I'd a skunk in my drawers. You understand my dilemma, Hobbs?'

'I can see how it'd put paid to all your plans, Mr Transome.'

'Exactly. Now I've been giving the problem some thought. As far as I know, the only ones with concrete proof of Jed's guilt are the marshal, his boy, the deputy and this schoolmarm. Take those four out of the picture, and my problem doesn't exist, does it, Hobbs?

'It sure doesn't, Mr Transome.'

'Good. Understand, Hobbs, I want my boy back unharmed. As to the rest, well, I'll trust to your initiative. Select three of your best men. Take care of this, and I'll make sure none of you wants for anything as long as you live.'

'Leave it with me, Mr Transome. The problem's good as taken care of.'

# FIVE

Alice Carnaby wiped chalk off the blackboard with a damp cloth and turned to face her pupils. Eight children whose ages ranged between seven and thirteen sat at pine desks facing her, fidgeting with books, slateboards and chalks as the minute hand moved to thirty after three. Alice looked at the clock and smiled. 'Wouldn't it be nice if you children were as keen to keep an eye on the time in the morning? Nobody would be late then, would they? OK, class dismissed. Don't forget your homework – everyone got their copy of *McGuffey's English Reader*?'

A chorus of voices rang out, 'Yes, Miss Carnaby.'

'Fine. See you all tomorrow. 'Bye, everyone.'

There was another chorus, 'Bye, Miss Carnaby.'

As the children ran across the yard, Jed

Transome left the shadow of a pinyon tree and walked to the schoolhouse. When he entered Alice was stacking slateboards on a shelf at the far wall, her back to the door.

'It's been a while since I had a look at *McGuffey*'s, Alice. Old Miss Tate was a good schoolmarm, but I reckon I'd a' learned a darn sight faster if I'd a teacher like you.'

Alice jumped, startled. 'Jed Transome. What – what are you doing here?'

'Come to see you, Alice. Don't have to make an appointment to see my fiancée, do I?'

Alice gave Jed a searching look. 'Jed, I told you plainly last time I saw you that we're *not* engaged. Why must you persist in this lie?'

'Oh c'mon, Alice, I know you like me, you told me so yourself on that picnic at Indian Rock.'

Alice sighed in exasperation. 'You're behaving like a backward child, Jed Transome. Don't you understand the difference between liking someone and loving them?'

'There's no call to be nasty, Alice. Ain't it true if you start out likin' someone you can get to lovin' them in time?'

Alice was curious if the marshal and his deputy had yet spoken to Jed. 'I did like you, Jed – in the beginning,' she replied. 'Your behaviour since,

49

however, has led me to despise you.

'Two days ago you had words with that French gentleman, Mr Bruille, who came to my aid in the storm. You were obsessed with this engagement nonsense then, and when he stood up to you, you threatened to kill him. This morning Mr Bruille was found shot dead on the trail just outside town. You were the one who murdered him, weren't you?'

Jed moved a pace closer. 'Ain't murder a kinda strong word, Alice? The guy was liftin' you, his Frog hands all over you – plain to see he was gettin' a kick outta it, too. Only natural to tell him to leave you be.'

'That's a lie. My ankle was sprained and all Mr Bruille did was help me on to his horse. To suggest otherwise is an insult.' Alice pointed to the door. 'Look, Jed, I'm not going to listen to any more of this nonsense. I want you to leave. I want you to leave this minute.'

'Oh, I'm leavin', Alice. I'm leavin' right now. And you're leavin' with me. We're headin' to Mexico, to start a new life. We'll get married down there, have us some kids, and live happy ever after.'

Alice said, 'Are you insane? I've told you I want you to leave. I've no intention of going anywhere with you.'

Jed took a firm grip of Alice's arm. 'I love you,

Alice, and I know you'll get to feelin' the same way about me sooner or later. Now, it'll be easier if you come without a fuss.'

Alice aimed a kick at Jed's shins, but he side-stepped and pulled her hands together in front of her. He drew her close and pinioned her arms between his right hand and hip. He then reached into his jacket with his left hand and brought out a length of cord. Alice struggled, but he managed to loop the cord over her wrists and bind them securely.

Alice was slightly winded by her efforts to resist. But soon she regained her breath and said, 'You're on the run from the marshal and his deputy aren't you? They know you're guilty of Mr Bruille's murder, don't they? And now you plan to abduct me. Don't you see you're making things harder for yourself? For goodness sake, Jed, let me go and give yourself up. Why allow things to get worse than they are?'

Jed stood back and surveyed his handiwork. 'Well, first off, Alice, I ain't abductin' you. I'm tyin' you up 'cause you won't see reason, that's all. But don't worry, sweetheart, I intend takin' good care of you. When we get to Mexico I promise we'll have a proper wedding, preacher and all, as befits a lady of your standin'.

51

'Second, yeah, it's true I shot that Frenchman, but only 'cause he'd designs on you and intended turnin' your head against me.

'You see, Alice, I know his kind. Them Frogs are good at sweet talkin' women till they get their way. You *do* know why he was comin' on strong, don't you, Alice? Why, he was after your virtue, sweetheart, pure and simple.

'Hell, it was plain as day to me he'd a come by your place on his way back from Dodge and taken it, too – by fair means or foul, trust me. I think you're special, Alice, thought so the first time I laid eyes on you. There was no way I could risk that Frog goin' anywhere near you again. I'd to put an end to his lecherous ways, once and for all, no choice about it. If that puts me on the wrong side of law, well, it don't matter none.

'Now c'mon, honey, I got a friend outside who's been readyin' your horse. He's goin' to Mexico with us, too. All of us gonna make a new start together.'

Louise Hayes had covered almost half the distance from the schoolhouse to her home when she discovered she'd forgotten her copy of *McGuffey's English Reader*. Ten minutes later she was approaching the school through a grove of pinyon trees when she saw her teacher and two men getting

52

ready to mount their horses. She was about to call out to tell Miss Carnaby she'd returned for the book when something made her stop. Looking more closely, the twelve-year-old realized something was wrong. The taller of the two men had a firm hold of Miss Carnaby, whose arms appeared to be tied in front of her.

The tall man lifted Miss Carnaby on to her horse and placed her bound hands on the saddle's horn. Louise heard him say to the teacher, 'Hold on tight, Alice. We've a good many miles to cover before sundown. We don't want you fallin' and sprainin' your ankle again, do we, sweetheart?' The two men then mounted their horses and rode off, one at each side of Miss Carnaby's Appaloosa.

Angus Bowman had ridden with General Sam Houston at the Battle of San Jacinto in 1836 when Santa Anna's army of 16,000 men was routed by Houston's 800 Texans. After the conflict Bowman moved to a reservation at Fort Towson in Indian territory near the Texas border, where he took up with a southern Cheyenne woman. Thereafter he became an Indian trader, and his son George was born a year later in July, 1837.

As more and more tribes were resettled, the Indian Nations became more populous. Over the next twenty years George grew up with the Indians, helping his father run the trading post, and in doing so became fluent in six tribal languages and more than a dozen sub-dialects.

George was also a naturally skilled tracker, and that and his language skills brought him to the attention of the US Army general commanding Fort Towson, who hired him as a scout.

In the mid-1860s there were frequent clashes between Indians and encroaching settlers. In central Texas in particular, the Comanches and Kiowa were a constant threat during and after the Civil War. George rode with US cavalry troops during this time, and his tracking expertise proved invaluable in running down renegades. His ability to speak most Indian languages was an asset, too, as it allowed the government to keep a channel of communication open with those tribal chiefs who were amenable to negotiation, and there were many occasions when this made the difference between bloodshed and peace.

By the early 1870s, however, military cutbacks caused George to be suspended from active duty, and although he received a nominal government stipend for retention of his services, most of his tracking work now came via the county sheriff's department, which employed him to help town marshals track fugitives from justice.

Such work was infrequent, however. These days George earned most of his living by working as an assistant at Cutter's Crossing's general store, and it was there Ross and Naylor found him on their way back from the marshal's house.

As the marshal and his deputy entered the store, Jeremiah Greenstock, the owner, greeted them with scant enthusiasm. 'I suppose it'd be too much to hope you fellas have come to buy somethin',' he said.

Naylor said, 'Well, first off, Jeremiah, let me say I hope you are well. But no, my old friend, you're right, we've come to see George.'

Jeremiah Greenstock was in his late sixties, with white hair and moustache. He was also bent with more than two score years of carrying heavy bags of provisions. He walked round from behind the counter and raised his hands in entreaty. 'Please, Abe, don't say you need George for county work. It's comin' up to my busiest time.'

Abe patted the old man's arm. 'I'm afraid so, Jeremiah. He here?'

Greenstock shrugged in grudging acceptance. 'He's out back, cartin' flour sacks from Mason's rig to the outhouse store.'

Naylor said, 'Go out and see him, will you, Hank?'

Ross opened the back door just as George was lifting a fifty-pound sack of flour to his shoulder from the back of a wagon. Bowman was well muscled and strong, and he carried the weight easily and without strain.

Ross said, 'Hi, George, how are you?'

Bowman turned, then hefted the bag back on the wagon. He walked toward Ross and extended his hand, his face breaking into a smile. 'Hank, my friend, I haven't seen you in months. I take it you're here on official business – about them drovers killed this mornin'?'

Ross shook his hand. 'Yes, George, I am. But it's still good to see you. The two men implicated in the murders are headed south. Abe and I followed their tracks just short of Pine Road, which leads south for another eight miles. As you know, the trail after that gets a mite tricky. Sage brush and such. Every chance of their tracks gettin' lost.'

'You know the men?' George asked.

'Yeah. Abe's boy and Jed Transome.'

Bowman whistled in surprise, then said, 'Stu Naylor?'

'Yeah, 'fraid so. Appears to have got mixed up with Jed, who we think is the killer.'

'You go out to Transome's place?'

'Yeah, but we didn't get to talk to Jed. He must've

seen us comin' and ran.'

At that moment Abe Naylor appeared at the store's back door. 'Afternoon, George. Hank tell you why we're here?'

'Yeah, Abe, two fugitives headed south,' Bowman replied. 'Sorry to hear one of them's your boy.'

'Yeah, well. But now we've got us a complication. Billy Hayes's been lookin' for us for the last half hour.' Naylor jerked his thumb over his shoulder. 'Just spoken to him in the store. His girl Louise saw Stu and Jed Transome over at the schoolhouse. They've taken Alice Carnaby.'

# SIX

There was only an hour of daylight left when George Bowman picked up the three tracks sixteen miles south of Cutter's Crossing. At this point the main trail south pushed into a valley with steep, pine-clad hills on either side.

For three miles the men had ridden back and forth several times. Then Bowman reined in suddenly and raised a hand. He pointed to an area of brush and said, 'The tracks go off the main trail here and to the left. They've headed into the high ground, up near the crest.'

Naylor said, 'Trying to throw us off the scent?'

'Seems that way, Abe. The tracks have zigzagged for the last four miles.' He pointed to the ground. 'See, there are three sets of tracks that go on from here and stay on the main trail, till they mingle with older tracks. I've been watching the brush and grama grass at either side, though. Looks like they've dismounted up ahead and walked the horses back over that. The broken brushwood indicates they remounted and moved off from here.'

Ross said, 'Ain't it rough goin' up there, George?'

'Yeah, mostly it is,' Bowman replied, then pointed to the top of the ridge. 'But from just below that high timber are a series of draws that run clear all the way down to Sutter's Falls – an old Comanche path. That trail's never far from cover on either side. We can track them, but we'll have a hard job spottin' them from any distance.'

Ross said, 'You think we've a chance of making the start of that trail before sundown?'

'Yeah, if we push on now, we might manage it by then,' Bowman replied.

'OK, let's go,' said Naylor. 'We'll set up camp for the night when we get up there. The horses could sure use a rest. Come to think of it, so could I.'

Hobbs and three of Elias Transome's other hands had been shadowing Ross, Naylor and Bowman for over an hour. The foreman and his men were less than a mile behind when Hobbs crested a rise and saw the marshals and the tracker stationary on the

59

trail ahead. He reined in, motioned the others to do the same, then dismounted and pulled his mount out of the line of vision. The men behind him also dismounted and the second rider, a burly man called Lane, strode over to Hobbs and said, 'There's three of 'em, Ev, who's the third – another deputy?'

Hobbs took a pair of field glasses from a pack on his bay and focused. 'No, a breed tracker, name of Bowman. He's pointin' up to the timber line. Jed and the others must've rode off trail.'

'There ain't no track goin' south from up there, is there?'

'There's an old Indian track just shy of the ridge. Winds all the way from there to Sutter's Falls.'

Hobbs had heard gossip in town that the Carnaby woman had run off with his boss's son. With Jed and the others ahead, and the breed tracker and the marshals in pursuit, he realized his mission was now all the easier. He added, 'We'll stick with the breed and the lawmen till they lead us to Jed and the others.' He sniggered and added, 'Then we'll have all our eggs in one basket.'

Hobbs saw movement ahead then, and adjusted the binoculars' focus. 'They're movin' off. Tell Bennett and Dawes to mount up.'

\*

Darkness had fallen when Jed and the others stopped for the night at a clearing eight miles along the Comanche trail. Stu got a fire going and made coffee, and Alice was massaging her wrists to get the circulation going when he offered her a cup. She accepted and sipped in silence, staring into the fire.

Jed said, 'Sorry to have had to tie your hands, Alice. There'll be no need for that now we're out here.' He walked to his horse, unhitched his war bag, then brought out a pair of Levis and placed them next to her.

'Here, when you've finished drinkin' that coffee go over behind them trees and change into these denims. They might be a bit on the big side, sweetheart, but they'll be a darn sight more comfortable than that dress.'

Alice stared at him coldly. 'Will you please stop calling me that?'

Jed grinned. 'Calling you what, sweetheart?'

Alice sighed in resignation and glanced toward Stu. 'You've hardly said a word since we started out,' she said. 'Why is a young man like you mixed up in this? Did you have a part in Mr Bruille's killing – are you on the run from the law, too?'

Stu didn't reply.

Jed said, 'On the run from the law? Why, his

61

pappy is the law, sweetheart. Say hello to Stu Naylor.'

Alice appeared shocked. 'Your father is Abe Naylor, the town marshal?'

Stu poked the fire with a stick. 'Ain't been no father to me.'

'What do you mean?' said Alice.

'Always threatenin' punishment, watchin' my every move, wantin' to know where I'm at most every time I see him – which ain't very often. Been that way since my maw died six years ago.'

Alice looked at Stu sympathetically. 'Jed told me he was the one who killed Mr Bruille. Why would your father want to arrest you?'

Jed laughed. ' 'Cause he was with me when I shot him, Alice. Stu didn't like the Frog any more than I did.'

'But he's only a boy,' Alice said. She looked at Stu. 'How old are you, seventeen? You didn't take an active part in the killing. I'm sure any court would award you clemency.'

Jed said, 'He's nineteen, Alice, a man. And as guilty as I am. You're in Texas, sweetheart, not Maryland. A man can get hung here for stealin' a horse.'

He paused. 'You're clever, though, I'll give you that. Tryin' to work in a little disagreement between

62

Stu and me, huh? Figure we'll get to fallin' out and take our eyes offa you? Well, it won't work, honey, Stu and me's pards, have been for years. 'Sides, there's nowhere to run to out here. Now take those Levis, Alice, and go and change. We've a long ride ahead, leavin' at sun-up. That dress just ain't suit-able.'

The embers of the fire glowed a dull red. Alice had difficulty sleeping, and lay awake listening to her captors' snores and the sound of the wind rustling through the trees. Every now and then she heard an owl hoot and the snap of brushwood being dis-turbed by some animal rooting around in the undergrowth.

Alice realized to make a run for it would be hope-less. For one thing, she had no knowledge of the country, much less of the heavily timbered area they were travelling through. She hoped the marshal and his deputy would pick up their tracks and follow, but couldn't help but worry that Jed's attempt to disguise their traces by criss-crossing back on the trail might have succeeded. She won-dered, too, if Jed would indeed make it all the way to Mexico and force her to marry him. Alice shud-dered at the thought, and soon drifted into a disturbed sleep.

She awoke with a start to see that dawn had broken, and it was then that she heard it: in the distance but unmistakable – the sound of gunfire.

As Bowman and the marshals prepared to move off after breakfast Bowman picked up on a small sound that he recognized from his past experience of tracking; it was a sound that put him on the alert. He said to Ross, 'There's someone following us.'

Ross turned from cinching his saddle. 'You think so, out here?'

Bowman threw the dregs of his coffee on to the fire. 'A few times yesterday I thought someone was behind us, but I wasn't sure. Then just a minute ago I heard something again that confirmed my suspicion.'

Naylor kicked dirt over the smouldering embers. 'Heard what, George?'

'It's a trick I learned when chasing renegade Comanches and Kiowas, back in '65. Often times a group of 'em would take to the hills, hide in the timber, try and throw us off the scent. Some of those woods were so dense there was little chance of pickin' up their spoor when you got into them.

'Anyhow, these Indians would hide deep in the forest and stand stock still on their mounts, never makin' a sound. We'd crash about after 'em for a while, then, thinkin' they'd outrun us, we'd give up and turn back.

'Then I remembered what an old hostler told me on the reservation. Take any bunch of horses and chances are that at any one time one of 'em'll have a cold – they get 'em same as we do. A horse's got big lungs, and when their noses get blocked they make a particular sound – a bit high-pitched, but if you're still, you can hear it over hundreds of yards. Well, listenin' for that sound is how I tracked them Indians. It's the same sound I heard yesterday – and again just now.'

Naylor said, 'How far away, would you say?'

'Four or five hundred yards, at a guess.'

Ross pointed to a rocky outcrop overlooking the trail. 'We could take cover up above that bluff, Abe, stake out the trail.'

Naylor took his Winchester out of its scabbard and racked the chamber. 'Right,' he replied, 'let's get to it.'

The rock shelf was thirty feet above, and over-looked the trail from where it entered the clearing. Ross had picketed their horses out of sight and now all three had their rifles at the ready, each with a good vantage point. Two minutes passed, then they heard the sound of approaching riders.

Ross thought there were three, maybe four men.

When the first came into view he immediately recognized him as the man called Hobbs he and Abe had spoken to at Transome's ranch.

Soon, Ross thought, the man and his companions would be in clear line of fire and would have no alternative but to give up their arms when ordered to halt.

It wasn't to be, however. Naylor chose that exact moment to raise his elbow to sight his rifle, and in doing so dislodged a fist-sized piece of rock, which crashed down the incline, alerting Hobbs. He and the three other riders reined in quickly, turned their mounts, and retreated back into the forest.

'Damnation,' Naylor said. 'Sorry guys, we almost had 'em in our sights.'

'Look, Abe, they've only retreated as far as the tree line,' said Ross. 'Did you recognize the lead rider? It was Hobbs, the foreman we spoke to at Transome's place. He must be after Jed.'

Naylor said, 'Why in hell's name is Transome doin' that? It's not his place to interfere. I'm gonna call 'em out.' He cupped his hands around his mouth and hailed Hobbs. 'Hey you – Elias Transome's foreman! This is Abe Naylor, marshal of Cutter's Crossing. I want you to come out here and state your business!'

There was silence for a moment or two then

Hobbs shouted back, 'Mr Transome sent us to look for Jed!'

Hank said, 'I don't trust him, Abe. Transome knows that's somethin' that should be left to us. He never offered men for a posse when we were out at his place. Seems to me he's got an agenda of his own.'

'What you gettin' at, Hank?' said Naylor.

'George here says Hobbs has been shadowin' us since yesterday. Why not come straight up and offer their help? No, they hang back and see where we're goin', then slink after us. Why? Because us not knowin' they're there puts them at an advantage, don't it? I think they know Alice Carnaby's with Jed, too. Think about it, Abe. You, me, Stu and the schoolteacher – each of us is the only ones with proof of Jed's guilt.'

Naylor said, 'You mean . . .'

Ross cut in, 'Yeah, wouldn't surprise me if those men are here to make sure that when we find Jed none of us lives to bring him to justice.'

Naylor shook his head. 'Well, if that's true it puts us in a tricky situation. We can't take 'em with us else risk a bullet in the back. On the other hand, if we tell 'em to go back, we know they just won't comply.'

Ross said, 'The way I see it, Abe, we've no option

but to ask them to disarm. If they won't do it voluntary, we'll have to shoot it out with them.'

Naylor said, 'Yeah, you're right, after the way he behaved at Transome's ranch, I wouldn't trust that Hobbs feller an inch. I don't see 'em givin' up their weapons, though, not without a fight.' He looked over at Bowman. 'Sorry, George – didn't reckon on getting you involved in no shootin' match.'

Bowman grinned. 'Don't worry, Abe. It won't be my first.'

Naylor turned and called out, 'OK, Hobbs, pay attention. Me and my deputy don't need no help in bringin' in Jed, you and your men are just goin' to be in the way. On the other hand, we don't trust you to go back, even if you gave us your word. Now, what I want you and your bunch to do is come out here into the clearing and surrender your weapons. You can get on your horses after, and head on home.'

Hobbs' answer was not long in coming. A bullet ricocheted off the rock above Naylor's head, and he, Ross and Bowman crouched low in response. Next, Hobbs and his men kept up a volley of fire from the cover of the trees that lasted for almost a minute.

Ross then heard their rifles being levered and reloaded. He rolled to the edge of the shelf and fired his carbine five times in succession across the width of the tree line. 'There's four of them,' he said. 'They're spread out, hidden in the timber. Abe, I'm gonna try and draw their fire towards me. You and George get a line on their positions.'

Like Ross, Naylor and Bowman had been firing in the general direction of the trees. Hobbs and his men were well hidden, however, and the smoke discharge from their rifles was obscured by the thick, coniferous canopy. Naylor moved behind a column of rim rock, and as he did so, saw a flash of orange in a stand of trees to the left of the trail. The bullet spanged harmlessly off the rocks behind him, and he saw another flash and returned fire.

'That big pine fifty yards left of the trail. See 'em?' Naylor said. 'Two shooters, about ten yards apart.'

All three then fired in the direction of the big pine and the trees surrounding it. Seconds later Hobbs and the others returned fire from along the entire width of the tree line. A hail of bullets stung the surrounding rocks, forcing the men to keep their heads down.

Bowman said, 'I can make out the muzzle flashes, Hank, but the fire's coming from changing directions. All four shooters seem to be moving about.'

'Trouble is,' Ross replied, 'this shelf's OK for shelter, but it don't give us enough cover for effective returning fire. We'll need to move back so as to draw 'em out.'

He looked along the rocky promontory. 'The shelf winds up there towards the edge of the bluff, then drops back into the timber just beyond where the horses are picketed. We need to get into the trees on the south side, where the trail picks up again. They'll be forced into the clearing to rejoin the trail. That puts them out in the open – just where we want 'em.'

# SEVEN

Naylor adjusted his position until he had the basalt pillar against his back. He pointed to the south side of the clearing. 'Hank, I've got the best position – I'll stay here. When I start shooting, you and George get moving. When you get there, keep 'em occupied until I join you.'

'Ain't that risky? All three of us can make it if we hug the path.'

Naylor replied, 'I know, Hank, but there's a good chance they'll see what we're doing and get to the other side first.'

'Yeah, you got a point, Abe.'

Naylor levered his Winchester. 'OK, on my word . . . go!'

Naylor moved around the column and began firing while Ross and Bowman hunkered down and started to move along the path. Hobbs and the others responded immediately, their rounds stippling the rock around the men's heads. Ten seconds later, Bowman made it to where the edge of the bluff merged with the surrounding hill. He dropped behind the crest and began returning fire. Meanwhile Hobbs and the others directed most of their fire at the rock shelf, forcing Naylor to take cover and fire sporadically.

Ross was just yards from safety, but then lost his footing – the shelf was narrow at that point and he scrabbled to retain a hold. Hobbs spotted his difficulty, and while his other men kept Naylor and Bowman busy, he and Lane walked into the clearing and concentrated their fire on his position.

A riot of bullets stung at Ross's heels and above his head; one of the rounds gouged out a sliver of flint that missed his neck by a hairsbreadth. Ross crouched immobile for a moment, then Lane racked his carbine and made ready for the kill shot.

Naylor glanced across and realized Ross's danger. He stood up, sighted the Winchester, and fired on Lane. The shot found its target and the burly man went sprawling.

The second he saw his sidekick felled, however, Hobbs became enraged. He elevated his rifle, pulled the trigger, and the shot caught the now-exposed marshal full in the chest. Naylor pivoted in surprise and staggered, then plummeted thirty feet to the ground below.

Ross joined Bowman behind the crest and fired at Hobbs, who darted back to the shelter of the trees. Bowman said, 'They got Abe.'

Ross was grim-faced. 'I know. I stumbled on the last stretch of path. He left his cover to shoot one of Hobbs' henchmen who had me in his sights.'

'There's still three of 'em, Hank,' Bowman asked. 'What do we do now?'

'I'm positive their plan is to get to Jed, Stu and the schoolteacher,' Ross replied. 'The fact Hobbs entered into a shooting match backs that up. I think Transome's ordered 'em to bring Jed back. The idea seems to be to suppress his guilt by getting rid of those with evidence.'

Bowman said, 'You really think they would stoop to killin' a woman?'

'Abe told me about Transome,' Ross replied. 'How he was mixed up in shady dealings over land contracts and property acquisitions when he came to town fifteen years ago. Two men who tried to expose him were shot dead in a gunfight one night. Transome's hands claimed the men had drawn first, but either there were no witnesses at the time or nobody was willin' to say anything.'

Ross paused and looked down to where Naylor lay. 'And now they've got Abe. But that still leaves Stu and Miss Carnaby. We've got to try and reach Jed before Hobbs does; once we get back on the trail and in the cover of the trees we'll be only a minute or so ahead. We need to put a greater distance between us.'

Bowman and Ross continued an intermittent exchange of fire with Hobbs and his men, who were still in the cover of the pines at the far side of the clearing.

Bowman said, 'I've an idea, Hank. There's a place where the trail forks about four or five miles from here. The Comanche path leads to the right side of a butte in the middle of a canyon, where it follows the Brazos river. The left side takes you over high ground. It's a rough track, but passable, and rejoins the Comanche trail four miles further on. It would give us a thirty-minute lead.'

'Could be the answer,' Ross said. 'I'll keep this bunch occupied while you get the horses. Abe's grey might give us a slight advantage: we can take turns forking it and spare our own mounts. I hate to leave Abe's body, though. I pray to God we're able to make it back and give him a decent burial.'

Minutes later Bowman and Ross were on their

mounts on the blind side of the bluff. They spurred the horses and galloped towards the south end of meadow where the trail picked up again. Ross called to Bowman, 'We'll be in their sights for less than a minute from the edge of the bluff, George. Keep your head down.'

At the other end of the clearing Hobbs heard the thunder of horses' hoofs. He leapt on his bay and shouted to the others, 'They're making a run for it. Mount up!'

The others did so, and all three raced towards the far side of the clearing. Hobbs and his men had covered a third of the distance when Ross and Bowman cleared the bluff and came out into plain sight. The pursuers then shouldered their rifles and began firing at the retreating pair.

Their galloping mounts made a bad platform, however, as most of their shots were wide of target. Of the three pursuers, Hobbs came the closest to a kill: one of his rounds hit the cantle of Bowman's chestnut, gouging a deep scar in the leatherwork.

Now under cover of timber, Ross and Bowman pushed their horses hard. After the first four miles Bowman's familiarity with the trail and its winding passage through a series of copses and draws gave the pair an advantage.

Soon they had gained a substantial lead on

Hobbs and the others and approached the canyon where the paths diverged.

'The fork's up ahead, Hank,' Bowman said. 'See, the Brazos river's on the right. The place where the trail veers off and follows it is to the right of that sandstone butte.'

'I see it,' Ross replied. 'Where's the track we take?'

'That grove of cottonwoods below the bluff to the left. Ride for the middle.'

When they came to the trees, Ross saw that a rough gravel-strewn path swung off where cottonwood trees blanketed a rise on the left side of the butte, an area hidden from view of the Comanche trail. He and Bowman took the path and in a few minutes gained the high ground where the canopy thinned and afforded a clear view below.

Ross reined his mount and motioned Bowman to do the same. 'Hold up a minute, George. Better make sure Hobbs and his men take the river road.'

Moments later they saw Hobbs and the others approach the fork. Hobbs didn't seem to notice that another path split away from the main trail. He and his men veered right and held to the route that followed the Brazos river.

Bowman said, 'Just as we hoped, Hank, he's sticking to the Comanche trail. It swings out and follows the course of the river for another ten miles and comes left again. Like I say, we go straight across from here and cut out ten miles.'

'Then we'd better get started, George, there's no time to lose.'

Alice's Appaloosa followed Jed's paint at a steady trot, with Stu's bay bringing up the rear. In the last hour the heavily wooded area they had been travelling through had thinned and given way to a largely treeless valley that followed the course of the Brazos river.

Alice was still thinking about the gunfire earlier that morning. The shooting had gone on for at least ten minutes, but she thought it might have been longer as she'd heard it from the moment she awoke. Jed and Stu had risen soon afterwards and got a fire going, and they'd all breakfasted on beans and bacon washed down with thick, bitter coffee. Neither man mentioned the shooting, so she assumed they hadn't heard it. Yet she knew it meant others were on the trail, and she wondered who it could be. She was jolted out of her reverie by Jed, who suddenly stood up in his stirrups and shouted, 'Smoke up ahead!'

Alice looked up and saw two men sitting by a fire on the other side of a bend in the river. Both looked to be in their late fifties or early sixties. One man, the thinner of the two, stirred a pot suspended over the fire by a hook attached to a wire frame. The other man crouched near the edge of the river holding a flat dish, the contents of which he swirled in a circular motion.

The men's horses were picketed in a clearing a few yards beyond.

As they approached, Alice saw Jed's hand stray to the butt of his pistol. The man beside the cooking pot stopped stirring then and looked up at him. 'Howdy,' he said. 'Pleasant day, ain't it? Miles and I are gettin' ready to have some sowbelly 'n' beans. We weren't expectin' company, but there's plenty in the pot. We'd be happy to have you and your friends join us.'

Jed looked at the man and his companion intently, taking their measure. Deciding they posed no threat, he said, 'Yeah, we've been riding for more'n five hours, I reckon we could use a break. You got coffee?'

'Sure,' the man replied, 'I'll put the pot on. Won't take but a minute. By the way, the name's Chester. Chester Oates – my friends call me Ches.' He thumbed in the direction of the man at the river. 'Yonder's my sidekick, Miles Giffney.' He turned and called out, 'Miles, vittles are ready, and we got company. Come 'n' eat.' He extended his hand to Jed then, and said, 'Glad to meet you, Mr. . . ?'

Jed shook his hand. 'Jed Transome. This here's my pard Stu and my fiancée, Alice.'

Stu and Alice were still on their horses and Oates went over to them. Alice offered her hand and Oates raised his hat in greeting. 'Pleased to meet you, Miss. You too, Stu. You all must be a mite saddle worn ridin' for more'n five hours. Please, come on over to the fire. Make yourselves comfortable.'

Giffney was a short, fleshy man with grey, mutton-chop whiskers. He sat on the opposite side of Oates and was introduced. Oates then ladled a generous helping of the stew on to four tin plates and passed them around. He took a fifth plateful and joined the others who were now seated by the fire. 'It's simple fare,' he said, 'but if I say so myself, I think you'll find it's OK.'

Giffney chewed a mouthful, swallowed, then motioned towards Oates with his spoon. 'Ches here was a cook on them big drives on the Shawnee Trail from San Antonio to Sedalia and St Louis back in the forties.'

'Yeah,' Oates said, 'Kansas City, too. Learned how to cook at my mammy's knee. Went north with some big outfits on the Shawnee 'fore they opened the Western and the Chisholm to Dodge and Abilene.'

Stu wiped his plate with a piece of pork. 'You outta the cattle business now?'

'Yeah, long time ago. Miles 'n' me stopped cow-punchin' back in '48. Two of us went to Californy, soon after Sam Brannan found gold in the American. Panned out there for better than seven years. Made us a fortune – and lost it too, didn't we, Miles?'

Giffney snorted and almost choked on a mouth-ful of stew. He downed it, then replied, 'Yeah, we fell prey to gamblin', drink and other temptations in San Francisco's Barbary Coast. Didn't take us but two months to get poor again.'

Jed said, 'And you're still pannin' for gold?'

Oates took the coffee pot from the fire and began pouring. 'Yep, 'bout the only thing Miles and me can do these days. Neither of us is fit to herd cattle no more. Ain't much of a livin' to be had pannin' either, but we get by. We live on the trail mostly, work the Brazos and the Colorado till we've got enough yellow dust, then take a trip to the assay-ers at Fort Worth. Then we get us some supplies, turn around, and start all over again.'

Alice said, 'Don't you have wives or families?'

'Had me a wife, Miss,' Oates replied. 'She died in childbirth in '41. The baby survived, though. My sister helped me raise him. He was killed at the battle of Chancellorsville in '63.'

'Oh, I'm sorry,' Alice said.

'Nothin' to apologize for, miss. It was a long time ago. Miles was married, too. Lost his missus back in '45. That right, Miles?'

Giffney cleared his throat. '1846,' he replied. 'Yellow fever. Didn't have us no children.'

Oates smiled. 'So, now we're a couple of old widow men passin' our days pannin' for pennies, but still dreamin' of strikin' it big.'

When they'd first encountered Oates and Giffney, Alice had considered the possibility of alerting them to the fact that she was being abducted. They were two old men, however, and she knew if she tried to make them aware of her plight it could put their lives in danger. She knew Jed would have no qualms about killing them.

In fact she was surprised that Jed had stopped at all; he must have considered the possibility of her trying to raise the alarm. It was a long time since breakfast, however, and she guessed his hunger had overcome any caution.

Yet he had made a point of placing a subtle emphasis on the word *fiancée* when he'd introduced her, and had caught her eye with a look that warned what would happen if she said anything out of turn.

'What about you folks?' Oates asked then. 'We seldom see travellers this side of the Western Trail.'

Jed took a sip of coffee then turned the cup in his hands. 'We're headin' to Mexico. Gonna buy a ranch. All of us are startin' a new life there.'

Oates studied Jed for a moment. 'Yeah, they say Mexico's OK. I hear beef's cheap. Property, too, I reckon.' Then, to Alice, 'You looking forward to it, Miss?'

Alice glanced at Jed. He gave her a cautionary look. 'I don't know much about it,' she replied. 'I've never been there. In fact, I'm a bit of a stranger to Texas.'

'Yeah, I thought that,' said Oates. 'Been tryin' to place your accent. You from back East?'

'Baltimore,' Alice replied.

'You meet Jed there?'

'No, we met in Cutter's Crossing, I'm a school-teacher there.'

Jed cut in. 'Was a schoolteacher, there. Alice gave it up when she decided to marry me, didn't you, sweetheart?'

Alice said nothing.

Oates stroked the stubble on his chin. 'Schoolteacher? That's a mighty fine callin', Miss.

And you came all the way out here from Baltimore to take it up?'

'Yes,' Alice replied. 'Miss Tate, the former teacher, was a friend of my aunt. She mentioned in correspondence she was retiring. My aunt told me, I wrote to the town council, and they gave me the appointment. I took over from Miss Tate in April.'

'And you're givin' it up after only three months to go to Mexico and get married, huh? Well, don't that beat all. Jed, you're a lucky young feller to have such a gal.'

'I'm not his ...' Alice realized what she was about to say and bit her lip. '. . . I'm sorry, I meant I'm not quite used to the idea yet.'

Oates looked closely at Alice. 'You've gone quite pale, Miss. Is anything wrong?'

Jed stood up then, and Stu followed his lead. 'It's the heat, ain't it, Alice? Makes you come over faint sometimes, don't it, sweetheart? Well, I'm grateful for your hospitality, gents, but I think it's time we were pushin' on.'

'Wait a minute, son,' Oates said, 'I was askin' Alice. You all right, Miss?'

Alice saw Jed's hand go to his gun belt. She rose and replied, 'Yes. Yes, I am thanks. Jed's right – it's the heat. Texas is a great deal hotter than Maryland. I suppose it's because it's much nearer the equator.'

Oates laid his cup beside the fire, got to his feet, and jerked his thumb in the direction of a tree. 'Ain't much after noon, Miss. 'Bout the hottest time of the day. If you're feelin' faint, I'd advise you to rest a spell. Old cottonwood over there gives plenty of shade.'

Jed's face took on a blaze of anger. He pulled out his revolver and pointed it at Oates. 'We don't need your advice, old-timer. You don't listen too good, do you? The lady said it's just the heat. We've got a long journey ahead, and she ain't got time to spend lying in no shade. Wasted far too long jawin' here as it is.'

# EIGHT

'Drop that iron, mister, else I'll blast a hole in your back.' While Jed had been preoccupied with Oates, Giffney had taken a Remington from a pack next to him. He now had it pointed at the young man's back.

'We may be old-timers, but we didn't get to be old by bein' stupid,' Giffney continued. 'You gonna do as I say, or do I pull this trigger?'

Jed scowled and dropped the gun.

Giffney then looked towards Stu, who was frozen in surprise. 'Now, you, mister – unbuckle your gunbelt and let it drop to the ground.'

Stu complied immediately. Oates then picked up his gunbelt and Jed's pistol. 'Keep 'em covered, Miles,' he said. 'I'll get some rope.'

Two minutes later Jed and Stu sat on the ground

together bound back-to-back, with their legs tied at the ankles.

Oates said, 'There, that should keep you from strayin'.' He turned to Alice. 'I'd a feelin' somethin' didn't sit right with that pair. Do you want to tell me what's goin' on, Miss?'

Alice pointed to Jed. 'That man's Jed Transome. He's wanted for the killing of a drover in Cutter's Crossing. He abducted me from the schoolhouse and forced me to ride with him. The other man's Stu Naylor, the marshal's son. I'm not sure if he's involved in the killing or not. I think Jed may have some sort of hold over him.' She paused. 'I'm so grateful to you for rescuing me. Thank you.'

'Ain't nothin', Miss. Why didn't you say somethin' sooner?'

'I was afraid Jed would try to kill you and your partner.'

'Well, that could've happened, I suppose. Miles'n' I are a mite long in the tooth these days. But that don't stop us allowin' for folks with evil intent. Either of us always keeps a pistol handy – ain't the first time we've been drygulched.' Oates scratched his head. 'Now we gotta figure some way of handin' these two over to the law.'

'I think there may be a posse trailing us,' said Alice. 'I heard gunfire before we left camp this morning. About thirty miles further back.'

Oates said, 'Gunfire, Miss? I don't think it likely a posse would shoot, not if they wanted to take these two by surprise.'

'We'll soon find out,' said Giffney, 'two riders approachin' fast.'

Ross and Bowman saw Alice with the two men and Jed and Stu sitting trussed on the ground. They reined in their horses and dismounted. Oates and Giffney stood next to Alice with their guns at the ready, regarding the riders warily.

Alice said, 'It's all right, it's the deputy marshal.'

Ross walked over and said, 'You OK, Miss Carnaby?'

'Yes, thank you. We stopped here an hour ago when these two gentlemen offered us their hospitality. We were on the point of leaving when Mr Oates here realized something was wrong. Jed pulled a gun on him.' Alice pointed to Giffney. 'Mr Giffney made him change his mind.'

Giffney extended his hand, then nodded towards Jed and Stu. 'Name's Miles, my partner here's Ches. You'll be takin' these men into custody, marshal?'

Ross shook the men's hands and introduced himself and Bowman. 'Matter of fact, we've got us a problem. Transome's foreman Hobbs and two other men are only thirty minutes behind us.

They've already killed Abe Naylor. I think they've been instructed to make sure none of us survives to take Jed back for trial.'

Alice looked astonished. 'Would Jed's father do that?'

Jed suddenly burst out laughing. 'Yeah, sweetheart, no doubt about it. You think I'm bad, Alice? You don't know my daddy. The man's a dyed-in-the-wool sonofabitch, if you'll pardon the expression.

'See, lately he's been mixin' with some real high-brow company. You know, power and influence? I hear those same folks are thinkin' of backin' him for governor. I'm guessin' he figures if I appear in court, he can kiss all that goodbye.

'That's why he's sent Hobbs. To take care of the problem.' Jed then puckered his lips and blew Alice a kiss. 'But there's no need for you to worry, Alice. Just say you'll marry me. I'll see nobody touches a hair of your pretty little head.'

Alice grew angry. 'I wouldn't marry you if you were the last man in Creation.'

'Then you'll just have to take your chances with the deputy, his breed sidekick and these two old-timers, won't you, honey?' Jed replied. 'Hobbs is gonna kill you all.'

Ross said, 'Shut up, Jed, or I'll gag you.' He turned to Oates. 'Ches, do you know this area?'

'Sure thing,' Oates replied. 'Miles 'n' I been trailin' these parts for years.'

'We need to find cover. Higher ground. Somewhere we can see Hobbs and his men approach.'

Oates thumbed over his shoulder. 'There's a big bluff a mile further on, narrow canyon behind it, mess o' big rocks in front. Reckon that'd do?'

'Sounds ideal,' Ross replied.

A short time later Bowman stood behind the rim rock at the edge of a wide depression thirty feet in front of a narrow canyon. Oates and Giffney were positioned behind a huge boulder on his right. Jed and Stu were handcuffed back-to-back around a large ash tree in the hollow near the canyon entrance. One set of cuffs coupled Jed's right wrist to Stu's left; the other his left wrist to Stu's right. Alice sat next to another tree up near the right side of the hollow's edge, where the horses were picketed.

Ross checked the handcuffs, then shouldered his rifle and walked over to Alice. 'The other men and I will cover the entrance to the canyon over by those rocks, Miss Carnaby.' He nodded to Jed and Stu. 'I've made sure those two's cuffs are secure. Any trouble, just give me a shout.'

'Thank you, Mr Ross.'

'Please, call me Hank.'

'OK, I will. But only if you stop calling me Miss Carnaby. My name's Alice.'

Ross smiled self-consciously. 'OK . . . Alice.'

As Ross started to walk away, Stu said, 'Were you with my pa when he was killed, Ross?'

Ross turned. 'Yes I was, Stu. Your dad saved my life. He was a brave man.'

Stu hung his head and looked at the ground, but said nothing.

'I don't know what part you had in Bruille's killing, Stu,' Ross went on, 'but I suspect whatever you did was influenced by Jed. It's my opinion you'll not face a murder charge.'

Jed yanked at the handcuffs and pulled Stu's arms taut to the tree. 'You said it yourself, Stu. You're an accessory after the fact. If I swing, pard, so will you.'

Alice looked at Stu. 'Don't listen to him, Stu. I've said it before, your situation's *not* irredeemable. Think about your father. He died trying to keep Transome's men from killing us. You witnessed Jed kill Mr Bruille. If you testify at his trial, it's extremely likely you'll receive a reduced sentence.'

When Stu didn't react, Alice added, 'Didn't you hear Jed say that Hobbs and his men will stop at nothing to prevent us testifying to his guilt? Think about it, Stu: you were there when he shot Mr Bruille. You're in as much danger as we are.'

Stu still said nothing.

'There's your answer, Alice,' Jed said. 'Stu and me's pards from way back. Ain't no way he's gonna say anythin' against his best friend.'

At that moment Giffney saw a cloud of dust on the horizon and called out, 'Riders comin'!'

Ross levered his carbine and sprinted over to join Bowman, who pointed toward the trail. 'See 'em, Hank? Just comin' outta the draw on the left.'

Ross nodded, 'Yeah, They've picked up our tracks. They're headed straight for us.' He called over to the prospectors, 'Hold your fire till they get nearer the bluff! We've got the better cover.'

'Don't worry, Hank,' Oates replied. 'We'll wait till we see the whites o' their eyes.'

Hobbs saw the sheer cliff ahead and reined in his bay. He waved his arm, signalling the others to stop.

'They're holed up in front of that big ridge. It'll be better if we picket the horses here and approach on foot. Bennett, you take the brush in the middle. Dawes, go left and use the cover of those trees. I'm gonna get in amongst that rim rock on the right.'

Bennett was a tall, reedy man with a drooping

91

moustache. He gestured toward the bluff. 'How d'you know they're there, Ev? You see 'em?'

Hobbs said, 'Don't need to see 'em to know they're there. That fire a mile back was doused recently. The tracks around it include a woman's footprints. There's also tracks made by at least six horses. It's plain to see the deputy and the breed's caught up with Jed. This is the nearest place with decent cover. Stands to reason they'd make a stand here.'

Dawes was paunchy, grey-haired and in his mid-forties. He said, 'Do you think they've seen us, Ev?'

'Yeah, ten to one they've been watchin' the trail. Couldn't help but spot our dust. Like I said, I want to make the best use of the available cover. When we're able to figure their positions I want you to listen. If I get any advantage I'll fire twice in quick succession. That means you keep shooting till I fire the same way again, or if you hear me say different. You got that?'

Bennett and Dawes nodded.

'Good,' said Hobbs. 'Let's get going.'

Ross watched Hobbs and the other two riders pull up and dismount just out of range. He then saw them all separate and move toward the bluff in different directions. He said to Bowman, 'Hobbs's guessed we're here, George. They're splittin' up. One of them's movin' through the scatter rocks on the left. The second's comin' through the brush. I think the other's in the trees to the right.'

Bowman said, 'I don't want to shout and give away our positions. I'll go over and tell the prospectors.'

'No need to tell you to keep your head down.'

Bowman smiled. 'You're right, Hank, no need.'

Bowman returned in less than a minute. 'Oates and Giffney are gonna keep tabs on the guy in the trees,' he said. 'I told 'em we'd watch the other two.'

'Fine,' Ross replied. 'It looks like they intend playin' cat and mouse. They'll have their rifles trained on the rocks and wait until they spot someone before shooting. We won't know where they're at till they do.'

Bowman said, 'Almost a Mexican stand-off.'

As Bowman spoke, Giffney shifted position and his head was momentarily visible. He ducked as a rifle cracked in the trees and a bullet spanged the boulder.

Ross said, 'Seems the stand-off just ended.'

Oates saw the rifle smoke drift from behind a solitary alder on the left side of a grove of birch trees. He crouched down at the side of the boulder

93

and returned fire.

Another shot rang out and ricocheted off a stone near Ross, who saw smoke rise from a group of rocks thirty yards to his left. He sighted the carbine, nodded in the direction of fire, and said to Bowman, 'George, there's a shooter tryin' to flank us on the left. I'll try and get him. You watch for any movement in that brush.'

Dawes then edged out from behind the alder and took another shot at the prospectors. As the round passed wide and hit the canyon wall, Giffney saw him move out for a moment and got off a shot in return. The bullet kicked up a fountain of dirt at Dawes' feet, making him duck back behind the tree.

Giffney then saw Dawes' shoulder exposed, and moved out from behind the rock to get a better aim. At that moment a shot rang out. The round caught Giffney high in the forehead, causing him to somersault before landing on the shale-strewn ground.

'Miles's been hit!' Oates exclaimed. 'The shot came from the brush.'

Ross looked over at the dead prospector. 'Damn,' he said. 'Ches, stay under cover! Don't take any chances! I'll see if I can draw 'em out.'

He had only just spoken when two shots were

fired in rapid succession. All at once the three men came under a sustained attack from the trees and the brush. The shooting was so intense it forced them to crouch low, and they could only manage to return sporadic fire.

The attack ended with two further shots, fired close together. There was a sudden silence and then Hobbs called out, 'Deputy Ross! I want to speak to you!'

Ross called back, 'What do you want?'

Hobbs said, 'You got somethin' I want, I got somethin' you want. I'd like to make a trade.'

Ross was aware that Hobbs was quite close. His voice came from somewhere over near the rim rock. 'What you got that I want?' he replied.

'Why don't you look to where your horses are picketed?'

Ross turned and looked over at the ash tree, then the awful truth dawned. He turned to Bowman. 'He's taken Alice.'

# NINE

'Hobbs must've worked his way around and taken her during that last volley,' Bowman said.

'It's my fault,' Ross replied. 'I shouldn't have let her stay so close to the edge.'

Hobbs called out again, 'You there, Ross?'

'I'm here,' Ross answered.

'I tried to take Jed, too,' Hobbs said, 'but you made a fair job of handcuffin' him. Just as well, eh, Ross? You'd have nothin' to barter with. Now listen. I'm gonna give you five minutes to hand Jed over. You don't, or try any funny business, this here schoolteacher takes a bullet. You understand?'

'I understand,' Ross replied.

Bowman gestured in the direction of the tree where Jed and Stu were shackled. 'You think he'll do as he says if you hand Jed over – set the teacher free?'

'Well, we've no alternative but to do as he asks for the moment, else risk him carryin' out his threat,' Ross replied. 'I ain't fooled, though; Hobbs's intention is to kill us all. This is just a spoiling tactic. Once he gets Jed, he and his men will try to finish the job.

'But I've an idea, something that just might give us an edge.' He thumbed in the direction of the canyon and called to Oates. 'Ches, does that canyon cut through to the Western Trail?'

Oates adjusted the brim of his slouch hat to cut out the sun's glare. 'Sure, Hank,' he replied, 'All the way through. The Comanches call it Squaw Pass. It's narrow, mind. Twists back and forth. Hard goin' for better than eight miles.'

'OK,' said Ross, 'here's what we do: I'm gonna unshackle Jed and take him up to the rim rock. I'll cuff Stu separately and leave him where he's at.

'Both of you watch out for Hobbs's sidekicks. When I get to the rim I'll ask Hobbs to make the exchange. If all goes well I'll get the horses and take Alice and Stu to the canyon entrance. When I get there I'll shoot once as a signal. When you hear it, both of you pull back and join me; I'll cover your retreat. Ches, after that I'd like you to escort Alice back to Cutter's Crossing and wait for us. If we don't make it back, send a wire to Marshal Terrell in Fort Worth.

'I don't plan on that happenin', though. George and I will find better cover in the canyon and set a snare for Hobbs and the others . . . there's no alternative but to come that way if he's to finish what he started. Once he's in, he'll find it difficult to manoeuvre. With luck, George and I should soon get the upper hand.' Ross paused and his face took on a determined look. 'I mean to recapture Jed and bring him to trial. But if all else fails, I'm prepared to shoot him and the others.'

Oates said, 'I'll make sure Alice gets back to town, Hank, you've my word on that. But, like George says, what if Hobbs tries to play you false at the handover?'

Ross nodded to the edge of the gully. 'Hobbs is on his own over there. I'll make sure Jed stays in my sights. I think Hobbs will give up Alice and wait till he's got a better hand. But if he does try anything, I reckon on shootin' Jed first, then him.'

Bowman nodded toward the brush. 'Don't worry about those two, Hank. They make any move, Ches and I'll plug 'em.'

Ross reached the hollow's edge with Jed walking

two paces ahead. He carried his carbine in one hand and a Colt .45 in the other, cocked and ready for action. 'OK, Jed, stop here,' he said. 'Make any move I don't tell you to make and I'll shoot without hesitation. You've my word on that.'

Jed had his hands cuffed behind him. He stopped, then glanced back. 'None of you'll make it, Ross, you know that, don't you? Hobbs won't let you take Alice back to Cutter's Crossing. And when I join him, I'll help make sure of it. I offered the bitch the chance of a new start with me in Mexico, but she turned me down. But I'm gonna make sure she lives to regret it.'

'You've run off at the mouth long enough, Jed,' Ross replied. 'Say any more and I'll shoot you now.'

Ross waited a moment, then called out, 'Hobbs! I've brought Transome's boy here as we agreed. Send Miss Carnaby over now. I'll uncuff Jed and send him back in return. But remember, I've gotta gun trained on him. Be advised if I see anything untoward, he's the first one to get a bullet.'

Hobbs stood behind a sandstone bluff thirty feet away. A flat expanse of table rock covered the area between where he and Ross stood. Ross saw Alice move out from behind the pillar, the barrel of Hobbs's rifle just visible and aimed in her direction.

'She's here, Ross,' Hobbs replied. 'Unharmed as

you can plainly see. Uncuff Jed and start him walkin'. I'll do the same with the schoolteacher. They'll be in clear sight of both of us all the way.'

Ross removed the cuffs. 'Right Jed, I'm gonna set you off . . . remember, measure your pace and pass Alice exactly at the midway point, stayin' six feet across from her. You move toward her, walk faster or start runnin' and I'll shoot to kill. You understand?'

Jed nodded.

Ross called to Hobbs, 'OK, Hobbs, Jed's comin'. Send Miss Carnaby over.'

Alice and Jed started walking. Jed's pace matched Alice's, and they passed each other almost six feet apart at a slight rise on the table rock.

'Go to your deputy, darlin',' Jed hissed from the side of his mouth. 'Won't be long 'fore you join him in hell.'

Alice gave a visible shudder, but said nothing and continued walking.

Ross saw that Jed had almost reached Hobbs, but Alice still had six yards to cover. 'Hurry, Alice, hurry!' he shouted. Alice ran and Ross grabbed her arm and pulled her out of danger. 'We're movin' into the canyon, Alice,' he said. 'And we've no time to waste.'

Alice had the horses' reins and was almost at the

canyon entrance when Ross went over to fetch Stu. The young man saw him coming and jumped up suddenly and broke into a run. His hands, cuffed at his back, affected his balance and at one point he staggered and almost fell, but he was mid-way between the canyon entrance and the rim's edge when Ross realized what he was doing. 'Stop, Stu, stop!' Ross shouted. 'Stay where you are! If you go out there Hobbs'll kill you!'

Stu ignored Ross. He kept going until he reached the open ground above the gully, then began yelling at the top of his voice. 'Jed, it's me ... Stu!' he shouted. 'Jed, it's your pard! Don't nobody shoot. Tell 'em, Jed! It's Stu Naylor, Jed's par . . .'

He didn't live to say another word. At that moment Hobbs's Sharps carbine roared from the left side of the rim rock. The high-calibre round hit Stu's chest with a force that lifted him clear off the ground and knocked him all the way back to the gully.

Ross signalled with a shot and covered Bowman and Oates as they pulled back to the canyon entrance. Bowman said, 'Sorry, Hank. Stu got past me before I had a chance to stop him.'

'Ain't your fault, George. Alice and I both tried to warn him, but he wouldn't listen.' He turned then, and addressed Alice and Oates. 'Alice, this canyon leads all the way through to the Western Trail. George and I are gonna find a spot further along and make a stand against Hobbs and the others. Meantime, I'd like you to go on ahead with Ches. He'll take you safely back to Cutter's Crossing. We'll see you when we back there.'

Alice looked astonished. 'But that's absurd, Hank,' she said. 'That would leave only two of you to face four armed killers.'

'It's gonna get a mite dangerous, Alice,' Ross replied. 'Naturally, George and I'll pick the best spot to make our stand. But once the lead starts flyin'. . . well, I don't want to put you in danger.'

Alice shook her head impatiently. 'In danger?' she replied. 'Don't you see since Jed abducted me I've been in constant danger? In this last hour alone Hobbs and his men have done everything in their power to kill us . . . not forgetting the three men they've murdered already. Do you honestly expect me to skulk away now, leaving just two of you to face them . . . and more than likely bring the tally to five?

'No, Hank, I'm sorry, danger or not, I won't run. Mr Oates should be here with you. I can help you make a stand, too . . . if you give me a gun and show me how to use it.'

Ross looked bemused. 'You're a strong-willed

lady, Alice, I'll give you that,' he replied. 'OK, you can stay. But there'll be no need for shootin' lessons. I reckon we'll manage without you havin' to tote a pistol.'

As the canyon wound westward it began to narrow, and soon Ross and the others found the sheer rock face pressing in on either side. They had been riding now for the best part of an hour and had not yet come upon a ledge or other deviation that gave enough cover. After a series of tortuous turns where the gap reduced to little more than the width of a horse, the canyon suddenly opened into a circular chamber some sixty feet wide and a similar distance across. At the canyon wall to the right stood three huge boulders, which lay almost parallel to the rock face and were upended like dominoes.

Ross dismounted and walked around each in turn, checking the cover it afforded. 'This'll do,' he said. 'There's good visibility from each of these rocks, and hardly a gap between 'em. More important, all give a clear line of sight to every part of the glade. We just have to wait till Hobbs and the others come through, and we got the drop.'

'What if they suspect a trap, Hank, and try somethin' else?' Oates asked.

Ross pointed to the cleft they'd just ridden

through. 'See for yourself, Ches. The only way is through that openin' ... and they gotta come in single file. There's no way up, around or across. The canyon's at least forty feet high on either side. We'll picket the horses further down the canyon. They won't see us here – the boulders give total camouflage.'

'It will be nightfall soon,' Alice said. 'What if we don't see them?'

'That's a good point, Alice,' Ross replied. He pointed upwards. 'We're lucky there, though. There's a full moon this week. Weather's been good, too, so the night sky oughta be clear. Maybe there won't be as much light as we'd like, but it should be enough to spot any movement.'

Bowman dismounted and placed his hand on the ground. He kneeled and pressed an ear against the earth. 'They're closer,' he said. 'About ten or fifteen minutes behind us, at a guess.'

He and Ross then walked the horses a hundred yards further on, picketed them, and returned to the clearing.

'OK,' Ross said, 'the horses are tethered out of sight, and if it comes to a stand-off we've enough water and jerky to see us through. Alice, I'd like you and Ches to get in back of that boulder closest to the clearing's exit. George and I will take cover behind the other two. When we hear them approach nobody make a sound. We want to take them by surprise.'

# TEN

Bennett led on a dappled grey, followed by Dawes, Jed and Hobbs. They'd been riding through a series of turns in the narrowing crevasse for over twenty minutes, and the growing oppressiveness was starting to get to the lead rider.

'These goddamned canyon walls are closin' in on us,' Bennett complained. 'There's barely room to walk the horses.'

'Ross and them others are in front,' Hobbs replied. 'This is the only trail. If they got though, so will we.'

'How far ahead d'you think they are, Ev?' Dawes said.

Hobbs took off his hat and wiped the sweat from his brow. 'Ten, maybe fifteen minutes.'

Jed had spoken little since Hobbs negotiated his

exchange with Ross. But now he said, 'Stu was with me, Hobbs. Just like he claimed. We were pards, why'd you have to shoot him?'

'Told you, Jed,' Hobbs replied, 'it was a mistake. From the scrub where we were I couldn't hear much. Saw him come over the ridge and thought he was one of Ross's men. Anyway, don't you think it's for the best? If Ross had his way, he'd've persuaded Stu agin' you. After all, he was with you when you shot that Frog.'

'Stu took an active part,' Jed replied. 'Helped me trail those drovers and loaded my Sharps. He was implicated, Hobbs, don't you understand? He would have said nothin'.'

Hobbs smiled thinly. 'You could be right, Jed. Pity . . . now we'll never know.'

Bennett turned and called out, 'Some kind of clearing up ahead, Ev.'

'Rein your horses,' Hobbs said. 'I want to take a look before we move further. We ain't takin' no chances. Ross'll be lookin' to get the drop on us, and I don't aim to let him.'

Hobbs and the others walked to where the crevasse ended and the clearing began. The foreman looked out first, his eyes sweeping the area. The second he spotted the three boulders on the right, he motioned to the others. 'Pull back, it's a trap,' he said. 'Ross's over by those rocks. He's got the trail covered from here clear to the other side. We even think 'bout ridin' through, he'll shoot us down.'

'You sure somebody's there, Ev?' Dawes said. 'I don't see or hear anythin'.'

Hobbs took a Winchester from his saddle boot and levered the chamber. 'That's the general idea, Dawes. You expect them to come out wavin' their bandannas?'

'Ain't there some way to make sure, Ev?' Bennett said. 'I'm not disagreein' with ya, but it seems mighty quiet to me, too.'

Hobbs sniggered. 'Hah! That's exactly what Ross wants you to think. You gotta put yourself in the guy's boots, Bennett. He knows we're trackin' him. You think he's gonna ride through this canyon, head on up the trail and back to town, knowin' we're behind intent on makin' sure he don't get there? No. He picks a spot in this canyon. Someplace with plenty cover. This spot. Them rocks give a clear view of the passage from here to where it narrows again over there. Anybody movin' through gotta be in the open for fifty feet or more. You wanna make sure they're there? There's an easy way to find out . . . stick your head out and get it shot off!' Bennett looked abashed. 'No, we'll wait,'

Hobbs continued. 'It'll be dark soon. We'll run one of the horses through. It'll surprise 'em, maybe draw their fire. I'll get a bead on those rocks then and shoot anyone that moves.'

An hour later the canyon was almost in total darkness. The moonlight barely penetrated to the canyon floor, and Ross and the others could scarcely make out shadows.

A little after eleven, Ross heard a scuffle at the entrance to the glade. He turned to the others and whispered hoarsely, 'George . . . Ches! Something's goin' on over there. Get ready!'

Bowman quickly raised his rifle and trained it on the narrow entry point. Oates had been half asleep, however. He shook his head and rubbed his eyes vigorously.

Alice looked concerned. She lowered her voice and said, 'Are you OK, Mr Oates?'

'Yes, miss,' he croaked in reply. 'Sorry, I must've drifted off.'

No sooner had Oates spoken when there was the crack of a whip and a horse ran into the clearing at full gallop. Ross strained his eyes and saw it was riderless. He was about to tell the others to hold their fire when Oates shouldered his Winchester and pulled the trigger.

The shot echoed like thunder in the confined space and caused the horse to rear suddenly and whinny in terror. The terrified animal came back on all fours and skittered for a moment, then steadied itself and bolted to the other side.

Rifle fire reverberated along the canyon again as Hobbs crouched low at the entrance and began to target the rocks. Limited cover and poor light hampered his accuracy, however, and all his shots were wide of target. Ross and Bowman returned fire immediately, their bullets stippling the narrow entrance and forcing Hobbs to duck out of sight.

'Hobbs whipped the horse through to draw our fire,' Ross said. 'He probably suspected we were here, but wanted to make sure.'

'I'm sorry, Hank, I didn't know nobody was forkin' the horse,' Oates said. 'Truth is, I was half asleep – my eyes were blurred.'

'Don't matter, Ches,' Ross replied. 'Hobbs is a bit more savvy than I gave him credit for. He knew I was lookin' for a spot that gave us the edge. When he stumbled into this glade and saw these rocks, he knew this was it.'

'What happens now, Hank?' asked Alice. 'Hobbs knows we're here. We've lost the element of surprise.'

'It's a stand-off, Alice. But we still hold the trump

110

card.' Ross motioned toward the narrow opening. 'Hobbs can't get to us, but he's gotta come through there. He can go back, of course. But I don't reckon on that. Nope, I'm sure he'll wait. After a while he'll get desperate . . . try somethin'. We've just gotta stay put till he does.'

Alice said, 'Can we do that, Hank? Wait it out, I mean? What about food and water? Do we have enough to last if it turns into a siege?'

'We got full canteens here with us,' Ross replied, 'filled at the creek before we came up the canyon. Jerky, too. Enough to last a day or two. Next water's at the Brazos river, on the Western Trail. I reckon this canyon exits near there 'bout three miles from where we're at. Remember, Hobbs got no advantage regards to water. He'd have taken it same place as we did. No, if anythin' it'll force his hand – and I think that'll be sooner rather than later.'

Alice moved slightly then and a shaft of moonlight caught her face. Ross pointed to some saddle blankets. 'You look exhausted, Alice. Why don't you get some sleep? Don't worry about Hobbs. I don't think he'll try anything again tonight. The rest of us'll each take a spell at keepin' a look out.'

Dawn was breaking when Hobbs decided his next move. He and the others had moved back thirty yards from the canyon entrance and each had taken a turn at watch. An hour before dawn they got a fire going to make coffee, and as the pot came to the boil Hobbs looked into the fire, deep in concentration.

When the idea came to him he rammed his fist into his open hand. 'Of course,' he said, 'that's it ... brushwood! It burns real easy, don't it? And there's a helluva lot of it growing in this canyon, ain't there? That glade where Ross and them others are is covered in the stuff!'

'Brushwood, Ev?' Bennett replied. 'Yeah, it's growin' real thick in there.'

'That's the answer, Bennett, don't you see? We'll set the brushwood in front of 'em alight and smoke 'em out!' He pointed skyward. 'Around noon, when the air gets heavy and stiflin'. Once the fire gets a hold the smoke'll be thick. It'll give us cover, too. You and Dawes can move through and target 'em from the opposite side. Me'n' Jed'll take care of this side. We'll get 'em the second they leave the rocks.'

'You plannin' on shootin' Alice?' Jed asked suddenly.

Hobbs gave him a searching look. 'You're still not smitten by that woman, are you, Jed?' he replied. 'Don't you realize what trouble she's gotten you into? Ain't you aware she don't care two bits about you? She couldn't make her feelings plainer.'

'We could take still take care of them others, Hobbs. But I could take Alice with me. Head for Mexico as I was gonna do 'fore you showed up. I know she ain't willin', but I think I might get her to change her mind.'

'You ain't thinkin' straight, Jed. What that woman knows could see you danglin' from a rope. There's no way you're gonna make her change her mind. What's more likely is that she'll shoot her mouth off, first chance she gets. C'mon, son, see sense – get over her. There's a heap o' other women out there.'

Jed didn't reply.

Hobbs turned to the others. 'Dawes, Bennett, strip some o' that brushwood and tie it together in bundles. We'll make torches, ready for lightin'. Come noon, things are gonna get hot for that deputy.'

Ross awoke to see the sun had risen. Since midnight Bowman, Oates and he had kept vigil in two-hour shifts. Bowman had taken the first watch until two, and he himself had been relieved at four by Oates.

He looked up and saw the old prospector standing at the side of the boulder covering the clearing entrance. Bowman was dozing nearby, his head on his saddle. Alice was also asleep, huddled under blankets at the rock on the opposite side.

Ross stretched his muscles and stood up. 'Everything OK, Ches?'

'Yeah, Hank, everything's fine. Ain't seen or heard a thing.'

'I reckon they must've pulled back aways,' Ross said. 'They'll be plannin' a move sometime today, though, I'm sure of that.'

'Yeah, Hobbs is one determined sonofabitch, ain't he?'

'Yep, that he is. Look, Ches, I didn't get a chance to say anything earlier. But I'd like you to know I appreciate your help. I'm real sorry about your partner.'

Oates eyes misted. 'Yeah, I sure will miss old Miles. Him 'n' me been through a lot together. Good times and bad. Drovin', pannin' for gold. Trailed this country from Kansas to Californy. Never figgered on partin' comp'ny that way. I'd like to go back an' bury him proper, Hank, when this situation's settled.'

'I'm gonna make sure you're able to, Ches, count on it,' Ross replied.

Bowman lifted his head from the saddle then and rubbed his eyes. 'Sunup already, huh? I must've slept clear through the minute I shut my eyes.

Anythin' happenin'?'

'Nothin', George,' Ross replied. 'All quiet. Reckon I'll get a fire goin' and make us some coffee.'

Ross set a fire and got the pot boiling. A few minutes later all four sat around the flickering embers, sipping the freshly brewed coffee from tin cups.

Alice pulled a stray strand of hair from her face. 'Do you think they're still out there, Hank? It seems so very quiet.'

'Yes, Alice, I do. I was saying to Ches earlier, I think they've pulled up the canyon apiece. I figure they'll make a move soon, though. We've got good cover here, but it ain't likely to put Hobbs off. He's out there OK, thinkin' of a way to come at us.'

'But surely there's nothing he can do, is there, Hank? You said it yourself, this entire clearing is covered from these rocks. It would be suicide for him and the others to come through here.'

'He's a desperate man, Alice,' Ross replied. 'And desperate men take chances. I've been doin' this job nigh on twelve years, and in that time I've seen men gamble their lives on the slimmest odds.'

'But surely Elias Transome is mad to go to these lengths to protect his bid for governorship,' Alice said. 'A sane man wouldn't think for a moment he could get away with murder.'

'The prospect o' fortune can do funny things to folks' heads, miss,' said Oates. 'Back in '49 I seen the truth o' that many times. Some o' them claim-jumpers in Californy would kill you at the drop o' a hat – even for a piece of worthless land.'

'You gotta remember things are different west of the Mississippi, Alice,' Ross said. 'Any one of them cities back East has more law enforcement than we've got in the entire state. More often than not, arguments in Texas are settled at the point of a gun.

'See, a lotta men come to Texas and find they can get what they want just by takin' it. I'm sorry to bring up religion, Alice, but out here the bible's teachin' that the meek inherit the earth don't apply. Oftentimes it's the other way – the strong do. Men like Transome have gotten so used to gettin' their way, they think they're above the law.'

'Yes, of course, you're both right,' Alice replied. 'I suppose I've lived a sheltered life. I've never given much thought to the dark side of human nature.'

# ELEVEN

After breakfast, Ross, Bowman and Oates checked and reloaded their weapons, then took up positions in readiness for the expected assault. Later, as the sun approached its zenith, Alice brought extra bottles of water. She gave a canteen each to Oates and Bowman, then offered one to Ross. 'There's six full containers left, Hank,' she said. 'Do you think that's going be enough? It's getting really hot.'

Ross took the canteen. 'Thanks, Alice,' he replied. 'Yeah, it should be. I expect Hobbs to make a move any time now. Like I said, he and the others ain't got any more'n we have.' He pointed to the sun. 'They're bound to be feelin' the heat, too. It must be 'bout noon, the hottest part o' the day.'

As Ross spoke there was a scuffling sound at the entrance. He and Alice looked across and saw

Hobbs, Jed and the other two men each appear briefly and hurl a burning torch towards them. All four landed in the scrub directly in front of the boulders. The dry brushwood was aflame in seconds, and as the fire spread, a dense, acrid yellow plume rose and began to fill the clearing.

'They're gonna try and smoke us out!' Ross shouted. 'Take off your bandannas and soak 'em in water. Cover your faces. Alice – use your scarf! George, Ches, watch that entrance – they're gonna try and rush us when the smoke thickens.'

Seconds later the heavy smoke had reduced visibility to just a few feet. Bennett and Dawes took advantage of this and dashed for the opposite side, firing their Colts from the hip as they ran. In the smoke haze Ross saw only the muzzle flash from their pistols and returned fire, levering his rifle rapidly between shots. One of the rounds caught Dawes in the chest. His body arched and he hit the ground just as Bennett reached the other side.

Meanwhile Hobbs and Jed kept up fire from the opposite corner. The thickening pall obscured their targets, however, making accuracy impossible.

But now, even with the wetted cloths over their mouths, the smoke at the boulders had become so dense that Ross and the others had difficulty breathing. Ross realized if they didn't move soon

118

they would suffocate.

He took a hold of Alice's arm. 'Crouch low, Alice,' he said. 'There's still some breathable air near the canyon floor. Lie there for a moment – I'm gonna try something.'

He turned to Bowman and Oates. 'George, Ches – follow me. There's a patch of earth to the left that's clear of brush. We can't make out much in this smoke, but Hobbs and the others can't see us neither. We'll snake across there and try and nail 'em.'

Dropping to a crouch, Ross, Bowman and Oates inched towards a clear patch of earth some six feet in front of the boulders.

At they did so, Hobbs darted across to Bennett. 'The smoke's so thick they can't see us,' he said. He motioned in the direction of the boulders. 'Stick close to the wall and work your way round. Jed and me'll approach from the other side.'

But as Bennett began to edge his way across, the thick smoke got to his lungs and he began coughing. Bowman, on Ross's right, swung around to pinpoint the sound and saw movement at the far wall. He sighted the rifle and fired; the bullet found Bennett's temple and he dropped like a stone.

'Good shootin', George,' Ross said. 'That leaves two of 'em.'

119

Hobbs and Jed were now halfway between the entrance to the clearing and the boulders. When Hobbs heard Bowman's shot, however, he realized it came from the front of the rocks, not behind. He and Jed lowered their rifles and began shooting in that direction. But heavy smoke still obscured the area, and the shots hit the ground several feet from where the men lay.

Then just seconds later everything changed when a downdraft blew into the clearing, partially dispersing the smoke. As the veil lifted, Ross looked to his left and saw Hobbs and Jed edging towards the boulders with their backs to the canyon.

Ross sighted his rifle and was joined by Bowman and Oates, who also saw them. Ross called out, 'Hobbs! Jed! You're covered – drop your guns. Now, else we'll shoot to kill.'

Jed immediately threw down his rifle and raised his hands. Hobbs, however, dropped to one knee and fired off three rounds before jumping to his feet and running for the rocks. Luckily for Ross and the others, his aim was erratic and his rounds missed. He had covered only a few yards when three more shots rang out, almost simultaneously. Each found its target: Hobbs spiralled earthwards, rolled a couple of times, then lay still.

Ross and the others got to their feet. 'OK, Jed,'

said Ross, 'get over here and keep your hands where we can see 'em.'

'Well, I reckon I'll go back and bury Miles,' Oates said. Forty minutes had passed since the showdown with Hobbs, and he and his men had been given a makeshift burial under a mound of loose stones. Ross and the others were mounted and ready to begin their journey back to Cutter's Crossing. Ross was astride his roan, with Jed cuffed and seated on his paint in front. Oates's grey mare faced back towards the narrow canyon.

'You're sure you've plenty water, Ches?' asked Ross.

'Yep,' Oates replied. 'Those three canteens'll hold me till I get to the other side of the canyon.'

'Take Hobbs and his men's horses with you. First settlement you reach, sell 'em for the best price you can get,' Ross said. 'Saddles might fetch a few dollars, too. And remember to drop in next time you're in Cutter's Crossing.'

'Sure will,' Oates replied.

Four hours after leaving the canyon, Ross and the others were riding through a wide valley when Bowman touched Ross's arm and pointed to a column of dust on their left. A group of men were

121

riding parallel roughly a mile distant.

'Comanches, I think,' said Bowman, 'They've kept pace with us for the last fifteen minutes.'

'A war party?' asked Ross.

'I'm not sure. They're getting nearer. I'll be able to tell 'fore long.'

The Comanches soon narrowed the distance to three hundred yards. Ross gave Bowman his field glasses. 'Take a look,' he said. 'Tell me if you think they're fixin' to attack us.'

Bowman focused the binoculars. 'No, I don't think so. There's four of 'em. Dog soldiers – a hunting party. They've got deer tied over two ponies in back o' them. I reckon they've gotten close to check our mounts. Lookin' to see if they've got the advantage if they decide to steal 'em.'

Ross reined his roan to the left and began riding towards the Comanches. 'Stay here, George,' he said. 'I'm gonna see if I can spook 'em.'

The Comanche leader was surprised to see the rider who sat tall in the saddle change direction suddenly and head towards him. As the man came closer, the Indian saw he carried the latest Winchester repeater and that his sidearm was a .45 Colt. He had observed two other men in the party and guessed they were similarly armed.

The Comanche decided he was at a disadvantage. He gave a whoop, lifted his rifle aloft, dug his heels into his pony's flanks, and the horse sprang away from Ross at a gallop. His companions followed in his wake, whooping in unison. The Indians retreated into the distance and disappeared as quickly as they had come.

When Ross rode back Bowman wiped sweat from his brow. 'I was worried for a second there when that Indian raised his rifle,' he said. 'And more'n a mite relieved when I saw 'em scat. You sure spooked 'em good.'

Ross said, 'Think they'll come back?'

'I reckon not,' Bowman replied. 'I hadn't expected to see Comanches this far north. Like I said, I'm sure they're a huntin' party. They've got heavy packs – a sign they're a fair distance from their tribe.'

'That's good to hear,' Ross replied. 'It'll be dark soon. The horses are winded. I'd like to make camp and rest for the night.'

Three miles further on Ross and the others came upon a meadow fringed with live oak trees. They made camp near a stream, and by the time darkness fell Bowman had a fire going and coffee on the boil. Alice greased a shallow pan with pork fat, then placed strips of dried bacon along the bottom. She scooped in a cupful of beans from a drawstring sack, and placed the pan on the griddle. A few minutes later an appetizing aroma drifted over the encampment.

Jed sat near the fire with his back to a tree, his hands still cuffed in front of him. Ross walked over and took a key from his pocket. 'We're gonna have supper, Jed,' he said, 'and I'm gonna take off those cuffs so you can eat civilized. I don't want you to talk, though, just eat. Remember – one wrong move and you'll be lookin' at the muzzle of my pistol quicker'n you can bat an eye.'

Jed didn't reply. Ross unlocked the handcuffs and took him over to the fire. He gave Jed a plate, sat down next to him, and Bowman and Alice took their places opposite.

Ross chewed a mouthful of food and washed it down with coffee. 'This is mighty tasty, Alice,' he said. 'After two days of jerky it's great to have a hot meal.'

'Amen to that,' Bowman added. 'It's real nice, ma'am.'

'Thanks for the compliments,' Alice replied, 'I don't often get to cook for others.'

She looked towards Ross then and motioned with her fork. 'Those Indians we saw today, Hank,' she said, 'are they still at war with the government?'

'They were a Comanche hunting party, Alice,'

Ross replied. 'There's still bunches o' them, and Kiowas that won't give up their lands. George reckons their main group is further south. I don't think we'll see any more of 'em here.'

Alice's brow furrowed. 'This area was once Indian territory?'

'Yes, ma'am,' Bowman replied. 'All of Texas was Indian land once. Thirty or more tribes roamed free between Kansas, Missouri and Mexico. A lot of 'em been moved to the Nations now. But Indians don't think anyone actually *owns* the land. They believe the earth's like a mother – you gotta respect and look after her.'

'And the ones that have been moved out – they've been resettled against their will?' Alice said.

'I reckon so,' Bowman replied. 'My father became a trader at Fort Towson in Indian Territory in 1836, a year before I was born. My mother was Cheyenne. She told me the government's been resettlin' tribes there since 1830.'

'I can understand why they would feel aggrieved,' Alice said. 'It doesn't seem right to leave a place where your people have lived for generations.'

'It's the story of this continent, I guess,' said Bowman. 'Ever since Europeans arrived they've been pushin' ever westward, takin' up more and more land. I suppose it can't help but lead to trouble.'

Jed threw his plate down and snorted in disgust. 'Just listen to that breed,' he said. 'His folks were livin' in caves when the white man came. Well, some o' them Indians are still cannibals. Any trouble they got they brought on themselves. We offered them civilization and made treaties with them. They tore them up. Now they're runnin' round wild, scalpin' women and children. General Sheridan got it right at Fort Cobb . . . the only good Indian's a dead one.'

Ross took the cuffs from his belt and snapped them on Jed's wrists. 'I told you to keep your mouth shut,' he said. 'I ain't gonna tell you again. You're goin' back over and gettin' tied to that tree . . . and if you even whisper, I'll gag you.'

As Ross moved Jed, Bowman turned to Alice. 'What he said about Sheridan was almost true,' he said.

Alice looked surprised. 'About the only good Indian being a dead one?'

'Yes, ma'am. I was with the US Cavalry as a scout and interpreter. In January '69 I was sent to Fort Cobb where a pow-wow took place between Sheridan and the chiefs of fifty tribes. When Toch-a-way – he was the Comanche chief – was introduced, I heard him tell Sheridan, "Me Toch-a-way, I'm a good Indian." I saw the general give him a glass-eyed stare, you know, like the Indian was loco? Then I heard him reply, "The only good Indians I ever saw were dead." '

Ross came back and sat down. 'I'm sorry about that, Alice. I took the handcuffs offa him to let him eat civilized. I might'a known he'd go and forget his manners.'

'It's OK, Hank,' Alice replied. 'I didn't pay him any mind. I can't speak for George, though. It was he Jed insulted with his bigoted comments.'

'Oh, I've got a thick skin, ma'am,' Bowman said. 'I been name-called all my life. It don't bother me no more.'

'Anyhow, it ain't true what Jed said about Indians,' Ross said. 'Our government's made things a whole lot worse in their dealings with them. Colonel Chivington, for one, started a heap o' trouble back in '64 when he killed more than 500 unarmed Cheyenne and Arapaho in Colorado.'

'I remember my aunt saying something about that,' Alice said. 'It was in the Baltimore papers at the time.'

'It was reported as the Battle of Sand Creek, ma'am,' Bowman added, 'but it wasn't no battle. Black Kettle, the Comanche chief, camped there with more than a thousand followers and raised a flag of peace. The Indians went to bed expectin' talks to begin next day. Instead, Chivington arrived at first light, encircled the camps, and opened up with howitzers. Those that escaped were chased for more'n five miles. Women, children and unarmed men, all cut down and butchered.'

'My God,' said Alice. 'No wonder there's such antipathy from indigenous peoples. Do either of you think there'll be peace?'

'Given time, Alice, yes, I think so,' Ross replied. 'Incidents like these lead to mistrust, though, and that makes for conflict. I reckon it'll be a while yet.'

# TWELVE

The next morning Ross and the others started back after an early breakfast. Ross reckoned they were now less than twenty miles from Cutter's Crossing, and he hoped to reach the town before dark.

It was approaching noon when Bowman saw a dark outline at the side of the trail. On drawing nearer he and the others saw a pack pony, a horse and its rider all lying in the brush. The two animals and the man were dead.

Ross and Bowman dismounted and went over to the man, who lay face down. Ross turned him over, then stood up and used his hat to wave away the flies that were starting to gather. Ross said, 'It's Guenther Hartmann. He's a photographer in Cutter's Crossing. I was speaking to him only two days ago.'

'Chest and head shots. Close range,' Bowman said. 'That stuff strewn over there by the pony. Looks like whoever killed him has been through his gear.'

'Yeah,' Ross said, 'seems the shooter brought down his horse and pony first, rode up and killed him, then ransacked his things.'

'Hank, you told me that a picture he took tied Jed to the Frenchman's killing,' Bowman said. 'You think Transome's involved in this?'

'Looks that way, George. See, the blood's not quite congealed. I'd say Hartmann was shot no more'n three hours ago. The tracks are fresh, too. Look like they lead to town. You agree?'

'Yeah,' Bowman replied. 'I'd say three, maybe four riders.' All go back in the direction of—'

He was interrupted by the sound of hoofbeats. He and Ross looked up and saw a cloud of dust half a mile distant, and a single rider closing fast. Both went to their saddles and lifted their rifles.

As the rider drew near, Ross saw who it was and lowered the Winchester. 'It's OK, George. It's Erich, Hartmann's nephew.'

The young man dismounted, and recognized Hartmann lying beside the trail. 'Hello, Mr Ross.' He nodded toward the body. 'My Uncle Guenther, is he dead?'

'Yes, I'm sorry, Erich. Someone shot him.'

'A fire started at the studio this morning,' Erich said. 'The premises were destroyed, all within the space of thirty minutes. I rode out to tell him about it.'

'This was soon after Guenther left?' Ross asked.

'Yes, just after six. A short time later I was making breakfast upstairs – we live above the studio – and I smelt smoke. When I went to investigate, I saw that the fire had taken a firm hold in the developing room at the back. Minutes later it spread through to the front. I got out just in time.'

'Was everything destroyed, Erich?' Ross asked.

'Yes. Negatives, prints, cameras, furnishings – all in ashes now.'

Ross put his Winchester back in the saddle scabbard. 'Did you hear or see anyone at the back of the studio before the fire started?'

'No. But I was helping my uncle load up his pack pony out front before he left. Someone may have started it then.'

'Did you pass any riders on your way out here?'

'No, Mr Ross, I saw nobody.'

Ross pointed to Jed. 'Those pictures you processed, Erich – the ones your uncle let me see the day before yesterday,' he said. 'One of them proves that that man's a killer. His father, Elias

131

Transome, knows your uncle gave me that picture. I think he set fire to Guenther's studio this morning in an attempt to get rid of evidence, then came out here and shot Guenther because he knew too much.'

'But you have the photograph, Mr Ross, isn't that enough evidence?' Erich asked.

'Yes, I've got it.' Ross nodded towards Alice. 'A witness, too. But Transome didn't plan on any of us makin' it to court. What's happened here today proves he's still tyin' up loose ends. And he ain't alone. Goin' by the tracks, there's at least four riders. If you didn't see 'em, Erich, they must still be out here somewhere. We'll bury your uncle, then you'd better ride back with us. It'll be safer.'

An hour later they had resumed the journey, and the horses began to labour as the trail rose steeply and pushed into timber-covered hills. After a few miles they crested a ridge where the trees thinned, revealing a valley on their left. Ross looked down and saw a narrow stream winding its way through the dense scrub at the far side. He turned to Bowman and pointed it out. 'Look, George, a fresh-water creek. It's about twelve miles to town. The horses were watered back at the Brazos, but we might just need more water for ourselves. I've three canteens near empty, I'll go down and refill them.'

'No, Hank, I'll go,' Bowman replied. 'That incline's pretty steep. Your roan might step in a gopher hole. My mare's good at sniffin' 'em out.'

'OK, George,' Ross replied. He pointed to where the valley rose to meet the trail a half mile further on. 'You can catch up with us at that grove of cottonwoods.'

When Ross arrived in the middle of the trees he drew alongside Jed, who was just in front. He took the paint's reins and brought it to a stop, then raised his arm to Alice and Erich, indicating to them to halt. 'We'll wait here, folks,' he said. 'George has gone to get water. We'll give him a minute to catch up.'

No sooner had he spoken when there was the sound of carbines being levered. A voice called out, 'Don't move, deputy! There's four of us, each with a rifle aimed at your heart. Unbuckle your gunbelt and throw it down. Your Winchester, too. Do it now . . . and do it slow!'

Ross did as he was bid, then saw Transome and three others leave cover and walk into the clearing.

'Now I want you to dismount and keep your hands in the air,' Transome said.

Ross and the others dismounted and all except Jed raised their hands. Transome nodded approval and smiled. 'It was mighty obliging of you to pull up, deputy,' he said. 'I thought we were going to have to shoot to stop you.'

Jed walked over to his father and glanced back towards the trail. 'There's a 'breed with 'em, Pa,' he said. 'Gone down to the creek back there to fetch water.'

Transome turned to his men. 'Norton, Davis – get them guns and take care of that half-breed.'

Norton and Davis picked up Ross's guns, then went over to where their horses were picketed. As they rode off towards the creek, Transome and the remaining man kept their rifles trained on Ross and the others.

'We'll just wait here a spell till my men get back.' Transome said. He nodded in Jed's direction. 'In the meantime, Ross, I want you to throw me the key to Jed's handcuffs.'

Ross reached into his pocket and pitched him the key. 'You're crazy if you think you'll get away with this.'

'Well, I've managed pretty well so far,' Transome replied. 'You see, Ross, I'm a man who trusts his instincts. It's a characteristic that's served me well. I'd a premonition Hobbs would foul up, and I've been proved right.'

'Him and his men murdered Abe and Stu Naylor,' Ross replied, 'and a man by the name o'

134

Giffney that tried to help us. Now you've added the photographer Hartmann to the tally. You really think you can brush all that under the carpet?'

'Ah yes, Mr Hartmann,' Transome replied. 'Unfortunately, he and his nephew were the only ones remaining that could link Jed to the Frenchman's killing. I wasn't sure about photographic evidence, of course. I had to make sure no prints or negatives survived, hence the fire.' He motioned with the rifle toward Erich. 'I missed our young friend here this morning, though. But I'm relieved to see he's with you. Now I can tie things up in one neat little package.'

# THIRTEEN

Bowman had filled the canteens and was preparing to mount his horse when he heard riders approach. He thought Comanches might still be in the area, and reasoned it wise to remain cautious. He led the chestnut into a brush thicket and clamped a hand over its mouth. 'Quiet, lady,' he whispered, ''til we see who this is.'

Moments later two men rode down to the stream and scouted back and forth along its banks. The first of the riders, a swarthy man with a moustache, dismounted and began to forage through the bushes opposite Bowman, parting the brush with the barrel of a Spencer.

The second rider, sallow-faced and with red hair, remained on his horse. He grew impatient and pointed to a clump of trees on the opposite bank.

'Try over there, Norton,' he said. 'Behind them cedars.'

Norton jumped over the stream, went into the trees, and reappeared a minute later. 'Nope, ain't nobody there.'

'That 'breed's gotta be somewhere. Jed told Transome he'd come here for water.'

Norton leapt back over the stream and mounted his horse. 'If he ain't here, he's somewheres else. We'll try further along.'

Bowman realized these were Transome's men and that Hank had been bushwhacked. Hank had said he'd wait for him at the grove of cottonwoods up past the creek, and that was where Transome must have set up an ambush.

The man called Norton and his companion were now out of sight, further downstream. Bowman led his mare to the place he thought least likely they'd check on their return – the clump of cedar woods on the opposite side of the stream. He would wait there until the men gave up their search.

He would wait there and figure a way to come to Hank's aid.

Norton and Davis gave up their search and rode back to the cottonwood grove fifteen minutes later. 'Sorry, Mr Transome,' Davis said, 'we've searched the creek from top to bottom. We can't find that breed anywhere.'

Transome looked annoyed. 'Well, he can't simply have vanished. Never mind, by the time he attempts a rendezvous, he'll find his companions have gone. We'll take care of the business in hand first, and deal with him later.'

He turned to Ross. 'So, that leaves you and your friends, deputy. Now, I'd just as soon shoot you here. But that would mean having to bury you – we can't risk someone coming along the trail and finding your bodies. No, we're gonna make it easier for ourselves. We're taking you to Nine Mile Gorge.' Transome paused and studied Ross. 'You know it, deputy?' he continued. 'A deep, timbered ravine three miles from here? Well, when we get there the three of you are going for a little walk.'

While Transome and the third man kept Ross and the others covered, Norton and Davis tied their wrists. A minute later they all mounted and headed in the direction of Nine Mile Gorge.

Ross realized that George would follow soon and attempt a rescue; if not somewhere along the trail, then certainly by the time they arrived at their destination. Ross was aware, too, he had to be ready when the tracker made his move. The red-haired man called Davis now rode immediately ahead of him, and he was flanked by Norton and another man called MacNamara. Alice and Erich rode side by side at his back, with the Transomes covering the rear.

Ross's hands were on his saddle horn. The fellow called Norton had tied his wrists with heavy cord, but although the binding was tight, he could manage some lateral movement. He thought if he could manage to wet the rope, he might be able to stretch it a little and work his hands free.

Looking down at his roan's shoulders, he saw the animal had worked up a significant lather. Ross slipped his fingers below the saddle horn and wetted them with the horse's sweat. He then twisted the tip of his left hand over the back of his right, working his fingers between the back of his wrist and the loops of cord. He did the same with his other hand in turn, until the ligature had been thoroughly lubricated.

All the while he kept an eye on Norton and MacNamara, but both men stared ahead impassively, oblivious to his actions. The mixture of saddle soap and sweat managed to ease the friction and soon, though his wrists were raw and chafing, he was almost free.

Just then they cleared the timber and Ross saw a slope to his left and the yawning chasm of Nine

Mile Gorge twenty feet beyond. A blue jay whistled noisily from the line of pine trees that followed the incline to the edge. Ross knew there was a drop of five hundred feet from that point to the valley floor.

'OK, dismount,' Transome said. He pointed to Ross. 'Right, deputy. I want you, the teacher and the German to walk to the edge. The three of you got a choice. You can jump or get a bullet. If you're found it'll look like an accident. If I've to shoot, well . . . what the hell. The buzzards'll probably pick you clean before anybody gets to you.'

'You're a cruel and callous killer,' Alice said. 'No wonder your son turned out as he did. The main influence in his life has been a father devoid of humanity.'

Transome looked at Alice with a pained expression. 'Quite a speech, schoolteacher, quite a speech,' he said. 'But you're wrong about me being the only influence in Jed's life. His mother Megan was a kind, gentle, hardworking woman. Both of us sacrificed everything in the beginning. We prospered, too . . . at least for a while. Then came the depression of fifty-seven, when the bankers called in my loans. I went from boom to bust in a matter of months. I saw the rich get richer and the poor – and I was among them, then – get poorer. I'd to sell my ranch and scrimp to get by. The worry of it killed Megan. She was only twenty-six years old.

'Humanity? Hell, those bankers showed us little humanity. My attitude to life changed the day my wife died. I came to realize fortune favours the strong, those who are prepared to go out and fight – yes, even kill – for what they want. No, school-teacher, when I want something now I let nothing stand in my way.'

'Then I pity you,' Alice replied.

'Schoolteacher, neither your pity nor your opinion is of importance. We've wasted enough time talking already. I want the three of you to go on over to the edge of that rim.'

Ross, Alice and Erich walked toward the gorge, their hands bound in front of them. When they reached the lip of the gorge Ross saw a narrow shelf of rock seven feet below. He turned to the others. 'Listen! I've managed to free my hands. I'm gonna jump down on to that ledge. Be prepared to jump after me. I'll catch both of you.'

'But they'll come over to check whether we've fallen, Mr Ross,' Erich said. 'When they see us there, they'll shoot us.'

'It's OK, Erich, George's over in them trees,' Ross replied. 'He's gettin' ready. I want us to be out of the line of fire when the shootin' starts.'

'Are you sure George is there, Hank?' Alice

asked. 'I didn't see anybody.'

'That blue jay you heard whistlin' when we arrived, Alice . . . It ain't a blue jay, it's George. In the past when trackin' we've used it as a signal to let each of us know where the other was. Now both of you get ready, I'm gonna jump.'

Ross kept his back to Transome and pulled his hands free of the cord. He walked to the rim and dropped down on to the ledge, then turned and held up his arms. 'Alice – you first.' Then seeing her anxious look, he added, 'Don't worry, I'll catch you.' Alice hesitated for a moment at the edge of the precipice, then jumped. Ross caught her and staggered, momentarily teetering on the edge. He quickly bent his knees and regained his balance, then set Alice down on the rock shelf beside him.

Ross gestured toward Hartmann's nephew. 'Now it's your turn, Erich,' he said.

Erich took a step forward and hopped off the rim. His heels caught the edge and he rocked unsteadily for a second. Ross caught his arm, then Erich righted himself and pressed his body to the wall. Ross dropped to one knee then and began examining slivers of stone scattered along the rock shelf.

'What are you doing, Hank?' Alice asked.

'Trying to find a sharp flint, Alice,' Ross replied,

'to cut the cords from your wrists.'

'No need for that, Mr Ross,' Erich said. He moved to one side. 'Look in my waistcoat pocket. I've a small penknife I use for trimming negatives.'

Ross retrieved the penknife and cut their bonds, then all three heard a loud birdcall from the timber near the cliff edge. Ross looked up and saw Bowman standing in the trees. The tracker motioned toward Transome, then pointed to Ross.

'Keep down,' he said. 'George's letting us know Transome and his men are on their way over. The shooting's about to start.'

Transome had seen Ross and the others drop out of sight on the slope above, and was suspicious at their apparent willingness to leap from the rim. 'Norton, Davis, go over there and make sure they've jumped,' he said. 'There may be a ledge. One thing's for sure – there's nowhere else they can go. If they're still there, shoot them.'

Norton was the first to reach the edge. He saw Ross and immediately sighted his rifle. The second he did so a shot rang out and caught his forehead, sending him toppling into the gorge. Davis reacted immediately, and was in the act of swinging his rifle toward Bowman when a second bullet hit him in the neck, killing him instantly. The force of the round knocked him back to the rim, and the hand that held his rifle lay just a foot from the edge. Ross jumped up, wrested it from his grasp, and scrambled back up to the slope.

Transome, MacNamara and Jed had dropped to the ground when Bowman started shooting, and now they saw Ross reappear and began to target him.

Ross crouched low behind Davis's inert body and returned fire. MacNamara jumped up and shot again at Ross, who ducked, levered the Winchester, and fired back. The round smashed into MacNamara's eye, blasting a hole in his head.

As the last of his henchmen fell dead, Transome realized his situation was irretrievable. He and Jed were crouched in the open without cover, and he could see Ross and Bowman's fire was both accurate and deadly.

'Wait, wait . . . don't shoot! We give up!' he shouted. He and Jed threw down their rifles and put their hands in the air.

Ross stood up and Bowman walked out from the trees, then both went over to Transome. 'Different now the odds are against you, huh?' Ross said.

Transome sneered. 'I'm not a betting man, deputy,' he said, 'but even I know when I've a losing hand.'

Ross turned to Bowman. 'Keep them covered,

George. I'll go and get the others.'

When he appeared at the cliff top, Alice and Erich were relieved to see it was him and not Transome's men. 'It's OK, folks,' Ross said. 'It's over. Transome's men have been shot. I've arrested both Jed and his father.' He extended his arm. 'Come on, Alice, give me your hand, I'll help you up.'

# FOURTEEN

The sun was setting as they rode into Cutter's Crossing and arrived at the marshal's office. Ross put Jed and his father in a cell, then went back outside to where the others were still mounted.

'I'm going over to the telegraph office to send a wire to Tobias Wilcox, the circuit judge,' he said. 'He's due in town next week. I'm sending another to county sheriff Paxton in Glen Rose. I'm assuming Abe's role as marshal till he gets here. George, I'd like you take the job of deputy.'

Bowman pushed his back his hat. 'Sure thing, Hank. I'll go and let Jeremiah know.'

As Bowman prepared to move off, Ross smiled and said, 'Break it to him gently, George. I ain't exactly top of his Christmas card list already.'

As Bowman rode off, Erich tipped his hat to Alice

and turned to Ross. 'I'll get in touch with my insurers about the fire tomorrow, Mr Ross. I'll take a room at the Fairmont Hotel if you need me meantime.'

'That's fine, Erich. I'll be in touch about the Transomes' trial when the judge gets here.'

Erich spurred his mount, and Ross went over to Alice. 'I'm sorry about the ordeal you've had to endure, Alice,' he said. 'Do you think you'll be OK for the trial next week?'

'Yes, I'll be fine, Hank. I'm grateful to you and George for saving my life.'

'When Paxton gets here I'm gonna leave him in charge for a couple of days,' Ross said. 'George and I promised to go back and bury Abe and Stu. When I get back do you mind if I swing by your place? Make sure you're OK?'

'I'm sure I'll be fine, Hank,' Alice replied. 'But please drop by. I'll be glad to see you.'

Two days later after the burials Ross got back to town. He left Bowman in charge of the office and rode out to see Alice, who had just dismissed her class when he arrived. She wore a bright yellow dress and her hair was tied back with a blue cotton ribbon.

Ross dismounted and smiled, then doffed his

hat. 'Howdy, Alice. I hardly recognized you. That sure is a pretty dress.'

Alice laughed. 'Makes a change from a filthy linsey-woolsey shirt and a pair of oversized denims, eh, Hank? I've got rid of the trail dust, too. Come on in, I've got coffee on the boil.'

A few minutes later Ross and Alice were seated in the kitchen, drinking coffee. Alice studied Ross's face for a moment and pushed back a stray strand of hair. 'You look worried, Hank,' she said. 'Is something wrong?'

Ross straightened up and put the cup on the table. 'The Transomes had a visit from their lawyer, Hiram Jackson. He spent an hour with them, spoke to me afterwards. Says they intend pleading not guilty.'

'Not guilty? Isn't that futile? The weight of evidence is against them, surely?'

'Well, Jackson says Jed's gonna claim Stu done Bruille's killin' because he wanted his gun. Transome senior is saying Hobbs acted on his own, he only told his foreman to bring Jed back. Jackson says Elias also denies involvement in Hartmann's death – and the fire.'

'What about me, Hank? Are they denying Jed abducted me in broad daylight?'

'I was comin' to that, Alice,' Ross replied. 'Jed's

gonna say you went with him willingly. Now you and I both know all this is a load o' hogwash. But we've still gotta prove them wrong. That Jackson's a slimy character, got a fancy way of twistin' words to make right seem wrong and wrong seem right. Abe and me seen a couple o' guilty men walk as a result of his double-talk.'

'The truth is still the truth, Hank. A duplicitous lawyer won't change that.'

'You're right, Alice,' Ross replied. 'Well, there's one good thing; we got an ally in the judge, Tobias Wilcox. He's a straight shooter. He don't take kindly to whitewash.'

# FIFTEEN

Five days later the Transomes' trial opened to a packed courthouse. On the front row on the left were Erich, Alice, Bowman and Ross, together with Andrew Taphill, the county prosecutor. Hiram Jackson sat next to the aisle on the front row to the right, with Jed and Elias Transome seated on his other side. Everyone rose as Judge Wilcox entered the court and went to the bench. He wore a dark suit, and was a short, middle-aged man with thinning hair. The jury – all men – sat on chairs placed in a line at right-angles to the bench.

'OK everyone, please be seated,' Wilcox said. 'My name is Tobias Wilcox, circuit judge representing Glen Rose County. The county prosecutor is Mr Andrew Taphill. The defendants are Elias Transome and Jedediah Transome, represented here today by Mr Hiram Jackson, and both father and son will be tried in tandem. How do your clients plead, Mr Jackson?'

Jackson rose and inclined his head in deference. 'Not guilty to all charges, your honour.'

Wilcox lifted a sheaf of papers from his desk and riffled through them. He took a pair of spectacles from a leather case, put them on, and consulted the first sheet. 'OK,' he said, 'we'll take Jedediah Transome first. Please rise, Mr Transome.'

Jed got to his feet and Wilcox peered at him over his glasses. 'Jedediah Transome, you are charged with the murder of Pete Bruille and Billy Temple on the 22 July 1874 to which you have pleaded not guilty. You are further charged with the abduction of Alice Carnaby on the 23 July of this year, and resisting arrest with the use of firearms. Your counsel has entered a plea of not guilty to all charges. Do you concur with your counsel's application?'

Jed didn't appear to understand the question. 'Concur. . . ?' he answered hesitantly.

Wilcox sighed with impatience. 'Do you plead not guilty?'

Jed turned at looked at Alice. 'Yeah,' he replied.

Wilcox gave him a stern look. 'Mr Transome, you will call me "your honour" and face forwards when you address the bench, do you understand?'

Jed looked slightly uncomfortable. 'Yes, your honour,' he replied.

'Fine,' Wilcox said. 'You may sit down. I'd now like to call the first witness for the prosecution, Mr Henry Ross, former deputy marshal and now town marshal.'

Ross approached the bench and was sworn in, then sat in the witness chair.

'Your witness, Mr Taphill,' Wilcox said.

Taphill was a rotund man in his late sixties with a tic that caused his eyes to blink continuously. 'Ah yes, thank you, your honour. Mr Ross, did you discover a photograph of Mr Bruille taken shortly before his murder showing him with a pearl-handled Deane-Adams pistol, later discovered to have been given to Stewart Naylor by the defendant?'

'I did,' Ross replied.

'And when you went to arrest Jed Transome, did he escape with the intention of going to Mexico?'

'He did. He abducted Alice Carnaby and made a run for it. We caught up with him on the old Comanche trail, fifty miles south of town. We arrested him there.'

'And when Elias Transome's foreman later forced you to give him up – threatening to kill Miss

Carnaby if you didn't – did he willingly join Hobbs with the intention of killing you and everyone with you?'

'That he did,' Ross replied.

Taphill turned to face Wilcox. 'No further questions, your honour.'

Wilcox nodded to Jackson. 'Your witness, Mr Jackson.'

Jackson walked over to Ross and waved towards Jed. 'Mr Ross, when you and Abe Naylor spoke to his son Stewart, he told you Jed had given him the Deane-Adams pistol, is that true?'

'Yes,' Ross replied.

'He said Jed had won it in a card game at Peacock's saloon, is that not so?'

'Yes, but Abe 'n' me found that not to be the case. Jed was nowhere near the saloon that night.'

'Precisely, Mr Ross. Stewart Naylor lied, didn't he?'

'Yes.'

'And when you accompanied Abe back to his house after interviewing Elias Transome, Stewart had vanished, isn't that true?'

'Yes.'

'In fact, he had joined Jed in his so-called flight from justice, is that not the case?'

'Yes.'

'Mr Ross, would you say that likely to be the reaction of an innocent man – to run, I mean?'

Ross shook his head. 'I'm afraid Stu was a bit easily led. He fell under Jed's spell. He was there when Jed killed Bruille and Temple. He ran because he was an accessory and was afraid of what would happen.'

'He may well have been afraid, Mr Ross, but for an entirely different reason. I suggest Stewart Naylor was Mr Bruille's killer, and the reason for the murder was that he coveted the Frenchman's revolver. He was so fixated on possessing the weapon that he persuaded Jed to keep a look-out when he went to steal the gun when the drovers were sleeping.

'The plan went awry when he and Jed arrived late to discover the men were on the point of leaving for that day's drive. Stewart then shot Bruille and took the gun. He was on the point of making his escape when the second man, Billy Temple, arrived. Stewart Naylor realized he'd been seen by Temple and shot him, too.

'The truth of it is that my client tried to restrain Stewart from carrying out the killings – but to no avail. It is Stewart Naylor who is the killer, Mr Ross, not Jed Transome. It is he who is guilty of the lesser charge, that of accessory.'

'That's horsesh—' Ross caught himself. 'I mean, that's nonsense.' He nodded in Alice's direction. 'Miss Carnaby was there when Jed threatened to kill Bruille.'

'Hearsay, Mr Ross, hearsay.' Jackson turned to Wilcox. 'Your honour, I intend to cover that point when I cross-examine Miss Carnaby. I have no further questions for this witness.'

Wilcox tapped on his desk with a pencil. 'Very well. Marshal Ross, you may step down.'

Alice was called next. She was asked to tell the court about Jed's unwanted attentions following their picnic at Indian Rock. Taphill then asked about the accident with her horse, her meeting with Bruille, and Jed's threat to kill him. The prosecutor concluded with her subsequent abduction and the events leading to her rescue.

The prosecutor then gave the floor to the defence.

'Miss Carnaby,' Jackson began, 'the ring Jed gave you, why didn't you return it?'

'I did return it,' Alice replied. 'I sent it back to him the day I received it.'

'My client advises me you didn't,' Jackson said. 'What's more, the fact that you didn't led him to believe you had accepted his proposal.'

'That's preposterous. I gave him back his ring. It

was accompanied with a note that made it clear I had no interest in his proposal.'

'Is that so?' Jackson said. 'I don't think you did, Miss Carnaby. In fact, I suggest that not only did you not return his ring, but when Jed suggested you go to Mexico with him, you went willingly.'

Anger flashed in Alice's face. 'That's utter rubbish,' she replied. 'He forced me to go with him. I tried to stop him, but he overpowered me and tied my hands. There was nothing I could do.'

'Wasn't there?' Jackson said. 'In that case, Miss Carnaby, can you tell the court why, when you came upon Mr Oates and Mr Giffney the day afterward, you said nothing to them about this supposed abduction? You didn't try to alert them or ask for their help in rescuing you.'

'I said nothing in the beginning because they were two old men. I was afraid Jed would shoot them.'

'Did he shoot them?'

'No, he didn't,' Alice replied. 'But he did become impatient when Mr Oates advised me to rest. He pulled a gun on him. Luckily, the man's partner, Mr Giffney, had him covered and made him drop it.'

'Was it not Jed's concern for your safety, Miss Carnaby, that made him anxious to move on? After all, these were two strange men, and you were in the middle of the wilderness.'

'No, that's not so,' Alice replied. 'Mr Oates and Mr Giffney offered us their hospitality. We stopped to have a meal.'

'Really?' Jackson said. 'I think as an Easterner, a native of Maryland, you may be somewhat naïve, Miss Carnaby. In much the same sense that you were naïve when Mr Bruille offered to take you home the day you were thrown from your horse.'

Alice flared. 'What do you mean?'

'Meaning your interpretation of his motives. My client was justifiably angry when he saw Mr Bruille lift you on to his horse. You may not be aware of it, Miss Carnaby, but Mr Bruille had quite a reputation as a seducer. I submit that you did not hear Jed threaten to kill the Frenchman, that he merely asked him to unhand you, and you interpreted that as a threat.'

'You couldn't be more wrong,' Alice replied. 'I don't know of Mr Bruille's reputation, nor do I care. All I know is he came to my aid when I was injured. He behaved like a perfect gentleman, and for you to suggest otherwise is an insult. It's Jed Transome who is the blackguard, sir. He killed Mr Bruille and then abducted me.

'When Mr Ross and the others came to my

rescue, he joined forces with Hobbs and his henchmen and made every effort to kill us, as did his father later on. Both men are liars and murderers, and your pathetic attempt to twist the truth here today is a perversion of justice.'

Almost as one, the spectators in the court rose and gave Alice a rousing ovation. People clapped, shouted, and booed at Jackson and the Transomes.

'. . . hear, hear! . . .'

'. . . you tell him, ma'am! . . .'

'. . . weaselin' shyster! . . .'

'. . . dirty murderin' skunks! . . .'

Judge Wilcox banged his hammer on its gavel. 'Silence!' he exclaimed. 'Silence in court.' He looked at Alice with a twinkle in his eye. 'A spirited reply, ma'am,' he said. 'However, there'll be no perversion in my court, of justice or anything else.' He turned to Jackson. 'You finished with this witness, councillor?'

Jackson had been taken aback with the outburst. He seemed flustered. 'Er, yes. Yes, your honour, no more questions.'

Afterwards the case for the defence all but collapsed. It was clear from the mood in the court that the citizens of Cutter's Crossing had lost patience with Hiram Jackson's feeble attempt to defend the Transomes.

The jury thought so, too. When Elias Transome stood, Jackson made the claim he'd only asked Hobbs to trace Jed and bring him home. The weight of evidence indicated otherwise, however. Ross and Bowman testified to the murders of Abe and Stu Naylor and Miles Giffney at the hands of Hobbs and his men. Erich and Alice added to the testimony, telling of Transome's admission of fire raising, his murder of Hartmann, and his attempt to kill them at Nine Mile Gorge.

The jury were out for only ten minutes and returned a unanimous verdict of guilty, and Judge Tobias Wilcox sentenced the Transomes to be transferred to the Texas State Penitentiary at Huntsville, where both would be hanged.

As Alice left the courthouse, Ross went over to her. 'Sorry Jackson put you through the wringer in there,' he said. 'I knew Wilcox would see through his whitewash, though. The townsfolk saw it for what it was, too.'

'It's OK, Hank,' Alice replied. 'I admit I got carried away for a moment. But I thought there was a chance they might get away with it.'

'Well, they didn't, Alice,' Ross said, 'and no small thanks to you.' He paused and put on his hat. 'But I gotta admit I'm glad it's over.'

Alice looked up at Ross. 'Me too, Hank.' She

walked over to her Appaloosa and unhitched the reins. 'I'd better get back. I've got a meeting of the parents' committee this evening.'

As Alice mounted up, Ross tipped his forefinger to his hat. 'By the way, Alice, I never got a chance to thank you for that coffee last week.'

Alice smiled. 'As I recall, Hank, you were so pre-occupied with the trial, you never finished it.'

Ross grinned. 'Would you mind if I swung by for a cup of coffee another time? I promise to drain every drop.'

'Why not tomorrow afternoon?' Alice said. 'School's out at three-thirty.'

'I look forward to it, Alice.'

As Ross watched Alice ride off, Bowman walked along the boardwalk behind him. 'Some lady, that Miss Carnaby, huh, Hank?' he said.

Ross turned to his deputy, the grin still creasing his face. 'That she is, George. That she most certainly is.'

2